09

Uno's Garden

Dedicated to Paul Gottlieb

Uno's Garden

Graeme Base

The animals go by one by one
a hundred plants, then there were none —
And all the while the buildings double . . .
this numbers game adds up to trouble.

But if you count with utmost care
(and trust me that they all are there),
you'll go from ten to nothing, then
the whole way back to ten again!

Abrams Books for Young Readers
New York

Uno arrived in the forest on a beautiful day at the very beginning of spring. There to welcome him were ten Magnificent Moopaloops, and one completely ordinary Snortlepig.

Uno loved the forest so much, he decided to live there.

10 Moopaloops

10 x 10 = 100 Plants

0 Buildings

. . . and 1 Snortlepig

Uno climbed above the treetops. The forest seemed to go on forever. Swinging through the branches were nine Leaping Lumpybums — and the completely ordinary Snortlepig.

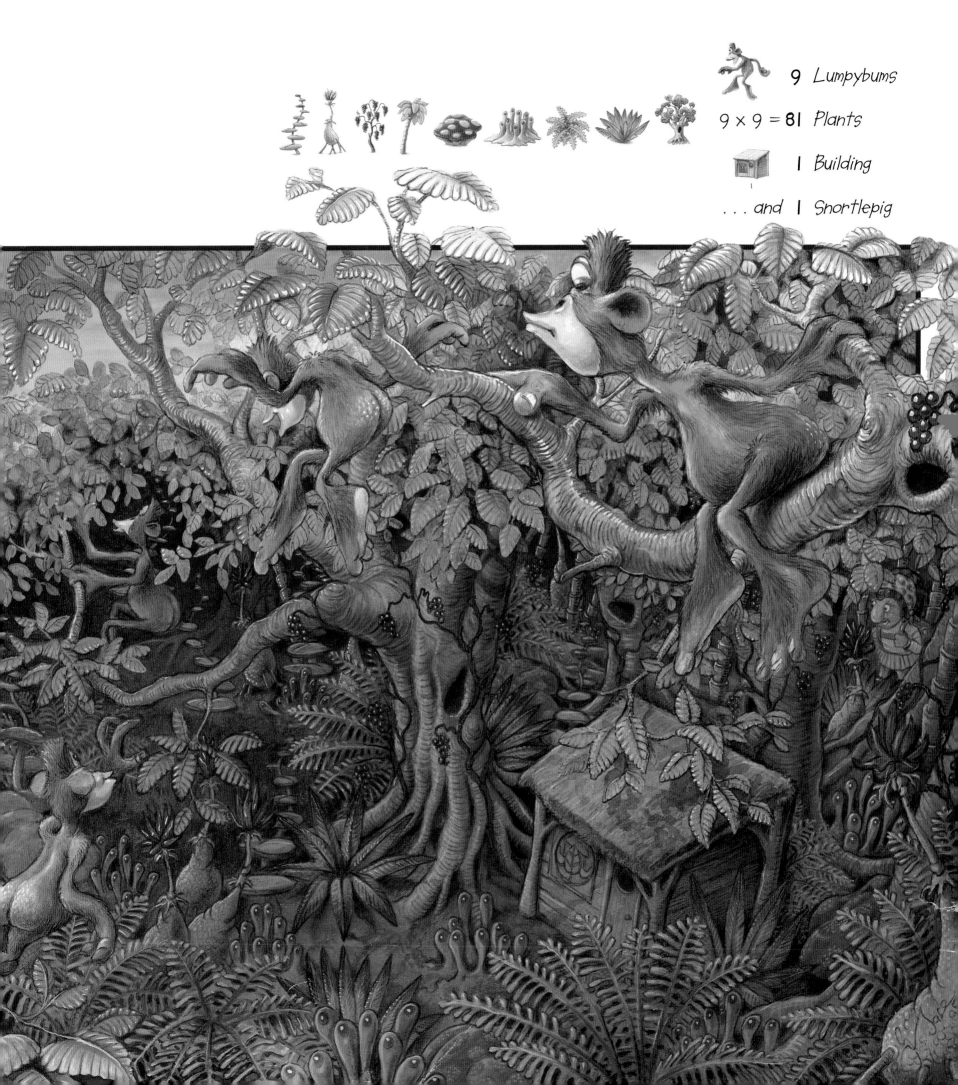

9 Lumpybums

9 × 9 = 81 Plants

1 Building

. . . and 1 Snortlepig

Others followed Uno. They loved the forest, too. They built houses and boats, watched by eight Feathered Frinklepods.
(And the Snortlepig, of course.)

Uno began work on a little garden.

8 Frinklepods

8 × 8 = **64** Plants

1 + 1 = **2** Buildings

. . . and **1** Snortlepig

The fishermen's children played games among the trees.
They counted seven Playful Puddlebuts, plus one Snortlepig.

A little village grew.

7 Puddlebuts

7 × 7 = **49** Plants

2 + 2 = **4** Buildings

. . . and **1** Snortlepig

Some hunters went into the forest looking for Sneaky Snagglebites.
There were six, but the hunters didn't catch them — or the Snortlepig.

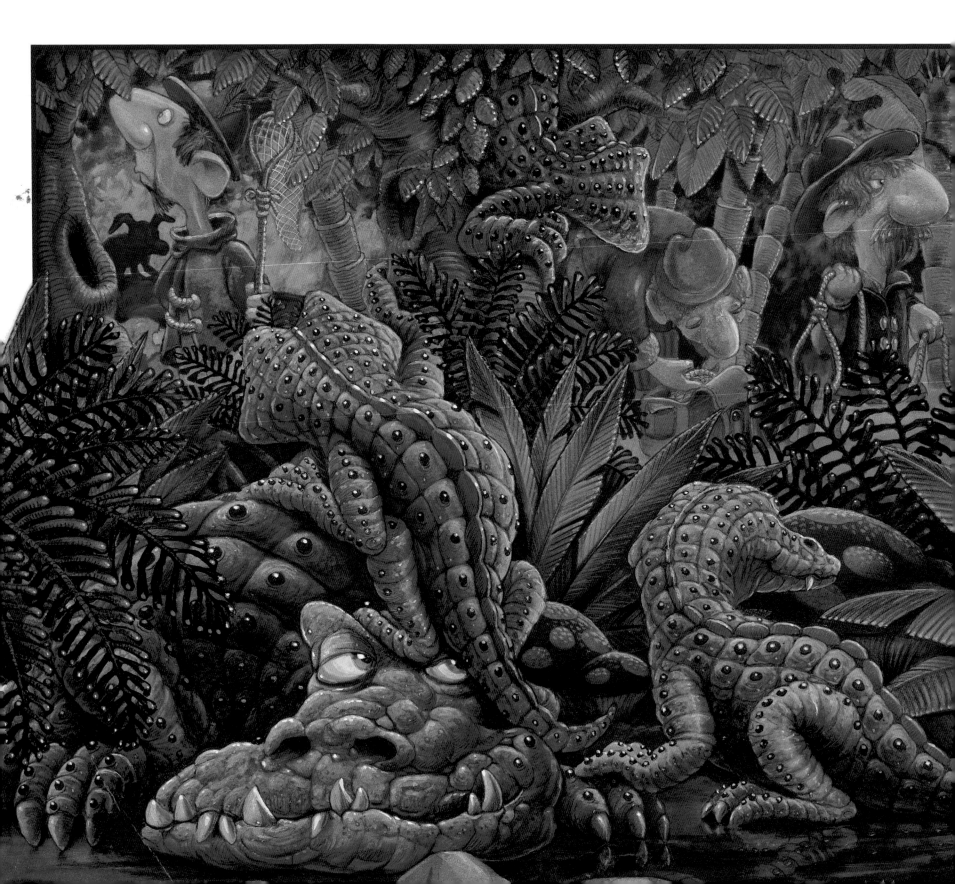

6 Snagglebites

$6 \times 6 = $ **36** Plants

$4 + 4 = $ **8** Buildings

. . . and **1** Snortlepig

Tourists came. They saw five Timid Tumbletops, but that was all.

Uno kept working in his garden. The village became a town.

5 Tumbletops

$5 \times 5 = 25$ Plants

$8 + 8 = 16$ Buildings

... and 1 Shortlepig

Then the railway was built. Excited passengers watched for wild animals. They caught a glimpse of four Grazing Gondolopes. And what was that other funny-looking creature back there?

4 Gondolopes

$4 \times 4 = $ **16** Plants

$16 + 16 = $ **32** Buildings

. . . and **1** Shortlepig

The town had become a city. A team of scientists arrived to study the animals. Three Flippered Flipperflaps was all they found.

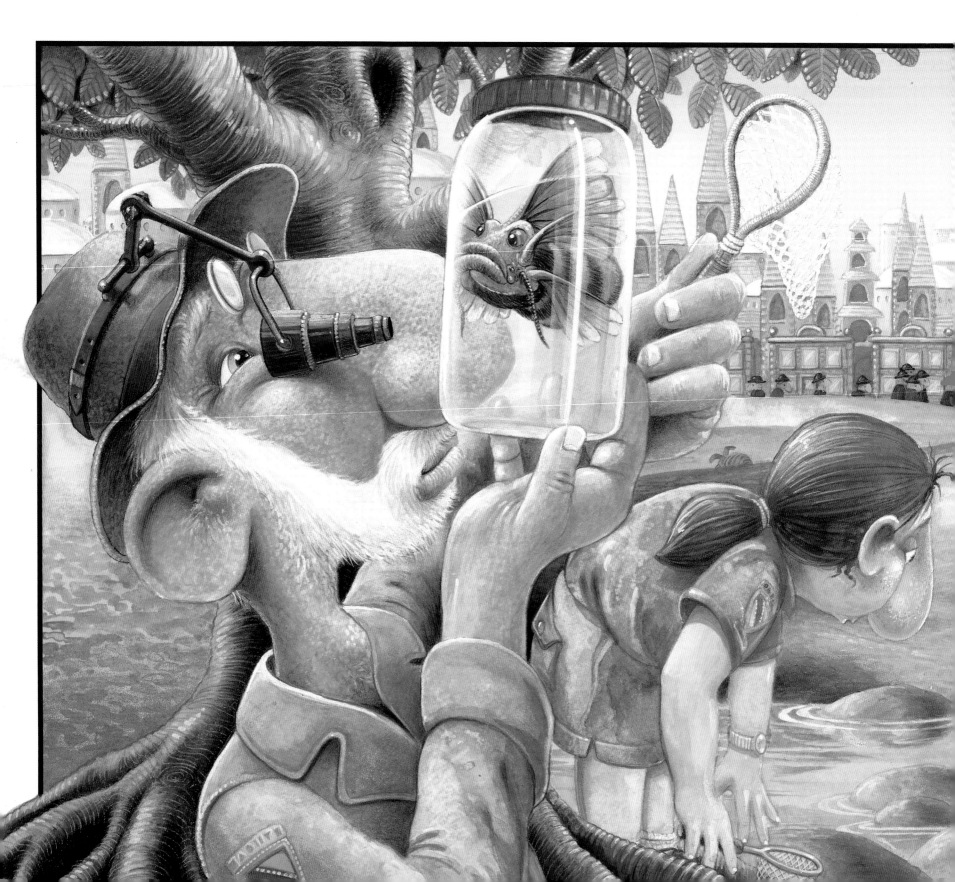

3 Flipperflaps

$3 \times 3 = 9$ Plants

$32 + 32 = 64$ Buildings

. . . and **1** Snortlepig

The city grew bigger and bigger and the forest grew smaller and smaller.

Some workers came across two Pointy Pricklebacks. They had never seen anything like them.

2 Pricklebacks

$2 \times 2 = $ **4** Plants

$64 + 64 = $ **128** Buildings

. . . and **1** Snortlepig

64   32   16   8   4   2   1   1

A lone fisherman set his line in the river. He caught a car tire, several old boots, and a cold. He didn't see the Snortlepig. In fact, nobody had seen one for so long, people weren't even sure they existed.

One gray morning, the people of the city woke up, looked out over the endless buildings, and were sad.

"Why do we live in a place like this?" they asked themselves.
"There are no trees."

So they left.

O Animals

O × O = O Plants

256 + 256 = **512** Buildings

256   128   64   32   16   8   4   2   1   1

The city was dark and abandoned.

Uno opened his door and looked out. Sitting there in the Garden, among the plants that Uno had saved, was a Snortlepig — completely ordinary in every way. Except that it was there.

The Shortlepig lived in Uno's Garden for many years.

The city crumbled, forgotten. The Shortlepig grew old and died. So did Uno. But the Garden lived on.

	Shortlepig
	Leefytree
	Old Shack

Uno's children continued to care for the little collection of trees and plants. And slowly the forest returned.

The children kept a diary of their discoveries:

Two Pointy Pricklebacks . . .

2 *Pricklebacks*

2 *Featherferns*

2 *Wigloos*

. . . but no Snortlepig

Three Flippered Flipperflaps . . .

3 Flipperflaps

3 Wiggleweeds

3 Log Cabins

. . . but no Snortlepig

Four Grazing Gondolopes . . .

4 Gondolopes

4 Bobblegrasses

4 Mountaintop Lookouts

. . . but no Snortlepig

Five Timid Tumbletops . . .

5 Tumbletops

5 Schmushlemushes

5 Gothic Mansions

. . . but no Snortlepig

Over the years, Uno's grandchildren added to the list:

Six Sneaky Snagglebites . . .

6 Snagglebites

6 Shadyblades

6 Mush Rooms

. . . but no Snortlepig

Seven Playful Puddlebuts . . .

7 Puddlebuts

7 Whynevines

7 Enviro-Habitation Pods

. . . but no Snortlepig

Their grandchildren added to the list, too:

Eight Feathered Frinklepods...

8 *Frinklepods*

8 *Trifflids*

8 *Houseboats*

...but no Snortlepig

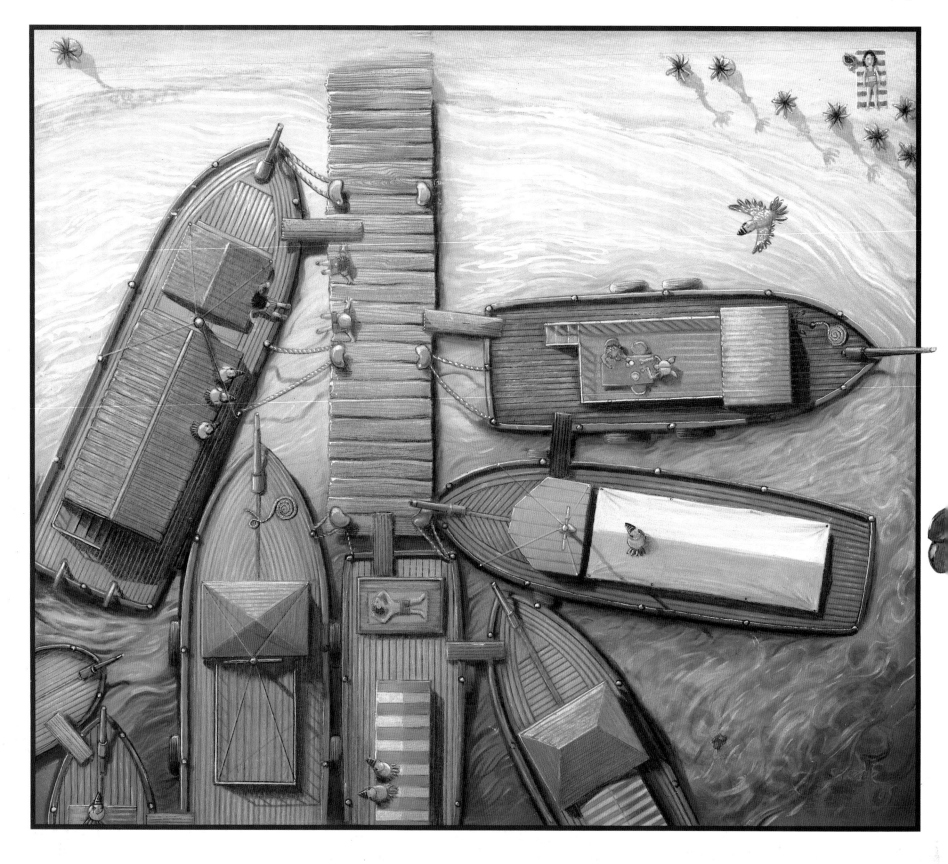

Ten Magnificent Moopaloops . . .

And on a beautiful day at the very beginning of spring . . .

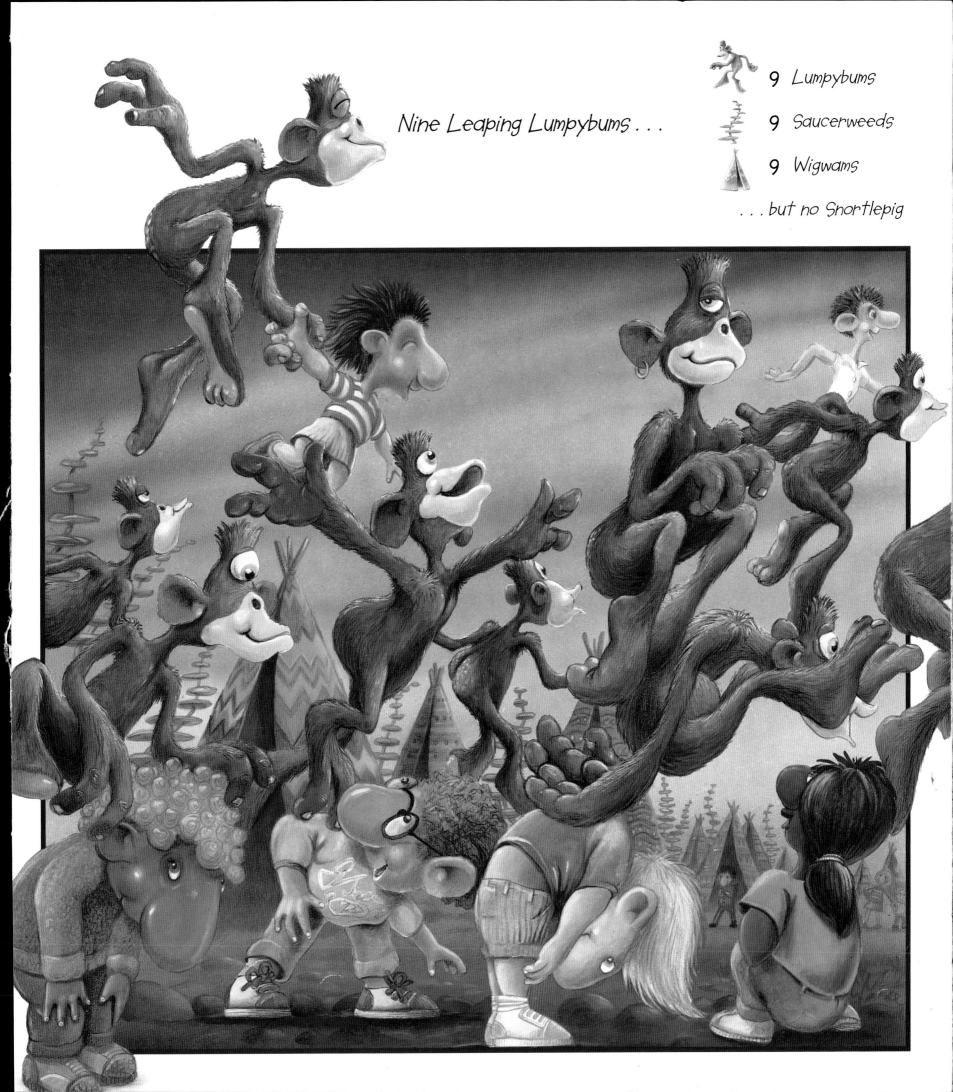

Nine Leaping Lumpybums . . .

9 Lumpybums

9 Saucerweeds

9 Wigwams

. . . but no Snortlepig

...the forest and the city found themselves in perfect balance!

10 Moopaloops

10 Sunnycups

10 Castles

. . .but no Snortlepig

Stories were told of the days when an extraordinary creature had lived in Uno's Garden. The children listened with wide eyes. And they never stopped believing that one day they would see a real, live Snortlepig for themselves.

Stories were told of the days when an extraordinary creature had lived in Uno's Garden. The children listened with wide eyes. And they never stopped believing that one day they would see a real, live Snortlepig for themselves.

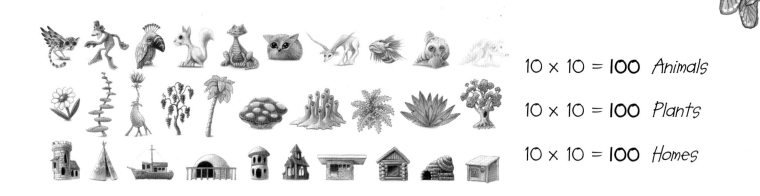

10 × 10 = **100** *Animals*

10 × 10 = **100** *Plants*

10 × 10 = **100** *Homes*

10 Moopaloops

10 Sunnycups

10 Castles

...but no Snortlepig

A Question of Balance

Getting the balance right is not always easy — especially between what people need and what nature needs — and it's surprising how quickly things can change when you're not looking! A gradual decrease on one hand, with a small but accelerating increase on the other, can add up to big differences.

The number games in *Uno's Garden* show how this can happen.

The **Animals Number Game** is the most straightforward: simple subtraction, one at a time — a steady countdown from ten to zero.

The **Plants Number Game** is another countdown, but this time in a reducing series of squares. (A square is what you get when you multiply a number by itself. For example, 3 x 3 = 9, so 9 is the square of 3.) Here we see big numbers getting smaller very quickly.

The **Buildings Number Game** shows what happens when numbers are doubled: a tiny increase at first, but quickly accelerating, resulting in dramatic change.

So when Uno's children have the chance to start over, they are very careful to keep the numbers game under control. Because in the end, it is all a question of balance.

By the way, if you're wondering about the number of people in each picture, in the first half of the book it's the first ten Prime Numbers*. In the second half, it's the same as the number of rediscovered animals.

---

* A Prime Number can only be evenly divided by itself and 1. The first 10 Prime Numbers are: 1, 2, 3, 5, 7, 11, 13, 17, 19, and 23. Curiously, if you add them all together you get 101. (But as 1 is sometimes considered not a Prime Number but a special number all of its own, that leaves us with exactly 100 — and makes Uno very much one of a kind!)

Library of Congress Cataloging-in-Publication Data has been applied for.
ISBN 13: 978-0-8109-5473-1
ISBN 10: 0-8109-5473-7

Text and illustrations copyright © 2006 Graeme Base

Printed and bound in China
1 3 5 7 9 10 8 6 4 2

HNA
harry n. abrams, inc.
a subsidiary of La Martinière Groupe

115 West 18th Street
New York, NY 10011
www.hnabooks.com

GOYA

MARIAROSA SCHIAFFINO

◆

ILLUSTRATED BY
CLAUDIA SARACENI
THOMAS TROJER

PETER BEDRICK BOOKS
NEW YORK

DoGi

Produced by:
DoGi spa, Florence
Original title:
Goya
Text:
Mariarosa Schiaffino
Editing:
Francesco Milo
Illustration:
Claudia Saraceni
Thomas Trojer
Picture research:
Katherine Forden
Graphic design:
Oliviero Ciriaci
Art direction and page design:
Sebastiano Ranchetti
English translation:
Anthony Brierley
Editing, English-language edition:
Ruth Nason, Nathaniel Harris

© 1999 DoGi spa
Florence, Italy

English language text © 1999 by
DoGi spa/Peter Bedrick Books

Published by
PETER BEDRICK BOOKS
156 Fifth Avenue,
10010 New York

Library of Congress
Cataloging-in-Publication Data
is available from
the Library of Congress
ISBN 0-87226-529-3

Printed in Italy in 1999

Photolitho:
Venanzoni DTP, Florence

♦ HOW THE INFORMATION IS PRESENTED

Every double-page spread in this book is a chapter in its own right, devoted to an aspect of the life and art of Goya or to one of the major artistic and cultural developments of his time. The text at the top of the left-hand page (1) and the central illustration are concerned with this main theme. The text in italics (2) gives a chronological account of events in Goya's life. The other material (photographs, paintings, and drawings) enlarges on the central theme.

Some pages focus on major works by Goya. They include the following information: (1) an account of the painting's history; (2) a description of the content and imagery of the work; (3) a critical analysis and detailed examination of its formal aspects. There are also reproductions of works by other artists, to set Goya's work in its historical context and demonstrate its originality.

CONTENTS

CONTEMPORARIES

Francisco Goya had a long and interesting life, lived during a turbulent period of history. Sustained by a profound confidence in his own talents, this painter from the provinces came to be admired by most of the leading figures in late 18th- and early 19th-century Spain; ultimately he achieved a stylistic independence that was rarely possible for artists at that time. Portrait painter to three generations of the royal family, Goya was also close to the intellectuals who attempted to reform Spain according to the principles of the Enlightenment or "Age of Reason." He was highly sensitive to the spirit of the Spanish people and their traditions. He painted scenes from everyday life, as well as extraordinary portrayals of the war in which his country was torn between the common people and the French army of occupation. But Goya's masterpieces were timeless, and the uniqueness of his genius meant that he founded no school and had no successors.

GIOVANNI BATTISTA ✦ TIEPOLO
(1696–1770)
Famous throughout Europe, this Venetian painter spent his final years in Madrid. Goya admired his frescoes for the Royal Palace.

GASPAR MELCHOR ✦ DE JOVELLANOS
(1744–1811)
Writer and reforming jurist, Jovellanos was one of the leading Spanish intellectuals, in regular contact with Goya during the years when the political debate was most lively.

FRANCISCO ✦ VAN DER GOTEN
Flemish by birth, Van der Goten was director of the Royal Tapestry Works of Santa Barbara in Madrid, for which Goya made dozens of preparatory cartoons.

JOSE LUZAN
(1710–85) A modestly gifted painter, Luzán took the young Goya as an apprentice in his workshop in Saragossa.

MARIANO GOYA ✦
(1806–74)
The artist's dearly beloved grandson, Mariano, inherited the "Deaf Man's House," his grandfather's last dwelling-place in Spain.

FRANCISCO GOYA ✦
(1746–1828)
The son of a gilder, Goya devoted his entire life to painting, changing artistic style several times but always with extraordinary results. He died in exile in Bordeaux. Only one of his children, Javier, outlived him.

THE DUCHESS ✦ OF ALBA
A fiery Spanish noblewoman, the duchess was one of Goya's great patrons. It is said that she had a love affair with him.

ANTON RAPHAEL ✦ MENGS
(1728–79)
After meeting the art historian Winckelmann in

Rome, this German painter embraced Neoclassical ideals. In Madrid he was First Painter to the King.

FRANCISCO BAYEU ✦
(1743–95)
Introduced to the court of Charles III by Mengs, Bayeu was later director of the Royal Academy of San Fernando. His sister Josefa married Goya.

MARTIN ZAPATER ✦
From their childhood in Saragossa, Zapater was Goya's closest friend. Goya's letters to Zapater provide important evidence about his life.

CHARLES III ♦
(1716–88)
Spanish king of the
Bourbon dynasty.
Duke of Parma and
King of Naples and
Sicily, Charles
acceded to the
Spanish throne in
1759 and embarked
on a policy of
reforms, with the
help of liberal nobles
and progressive
intellectuals.

CHARLES IV ♦
(1748–1819)
Succeeding his father
on the eve of the
French Revolution,
Charles IV became a
pawn in the hands of
Napoleon. Before
that, his wife **MARIA
LUISA** (1754–1819)
governed the state.
Her son **FERDINAND
VII** (1784–1833)
came to the throne in
1814, after the fall
of Napoleon.

**THE INFANTE ♦
DON LUIS**
The younger brother
of Charles III. At the
age of almost fifty,
Don Luis married
**MARIA TERESA DE
VALLABRIGA** (1759–
1833), who was not of
a noble family – so
her children lost any
right to the succession.
She admired Goya and
had a famous portrait
made of herself with
her entire family.

MANUEL GODOY ♦
(1767–1851)
Minister, and
favorite of Queen
María Luisa.
He was effectively
the chief minister
of Spain from the
1790s until
about 1805.
Godoy married
the **COUNTESS OF
CHINCHON**
(1779–1824),
daughter of the
Infante Don Luis.

SARAGOSSA

Saragossa is the capital of Aragon, a region in the northeast of Spain. The city lies in a plain on the right bank of the Ebro River. Originally a Phoenician settlement, it was later a Roman colony and then the capital of an Arab state. In the Middle Ages it became the seat of the kings of Aragon, which was united with Castille in 1469 by the marriage of King Ferdinand of Aragon and Queen Isabella of Castille. This event effectively created the kingdom of Spain. During the 18th century, when Goya began his artistic career, Saragossa's cultural and religious center was the great cathedral of El Pilar. Built in the 17th century and enlarged many times, the cathedral attracted many church-goers and pilgrims, and many artists and craftsmen who were employed to restore and decorate it. The young Goya was influenced by the art he saw there, which was inspired by the grandly dramatic Italian Baroque.

♦ EL PILAR
The cathedral is crowned by a large central dome, four corner towers, and ten smaller domes. It stands on the site of a shrine dedicated to the Virgin Mary that was built around a pillar (Spanish "pilar") on which, in A.D. 40, the Virgin is said to have appeared to St. James. In 1753 Antonio Gonzàlez Velázquez completed the spectacular fresco decoration of the dome in El Pilar's chapel of Our Lady of the Pillar. It is a superb piece of workmanship, painted some 130 feet (40 m) above ground level.

♦ THE HOUSE WHERE GOYA WAS BORN
When Francisco Goya was born, his family was living temporarily in the humble dwelling of his mother, Gracia Lucientes, in the country village of Fuendetodos. Francisco was the third of five children.

♦ OUR LADY OF THE PILLAR
Around 1760 this chapel of the cathedral looked like a building site. The chapel has three naves, divided by square pillars that support wide vaults and domes.

THE RETABLE ♦ OF THE HIGH ALTAR
The main nave is dominated by the ornate Gothic retable, or altarpiece, with painted and sculpted scenes from the life of the Virgin.

◆ **VIEW OF**
SARAGOSSA
Prado, Madrid.
The great Spanish
painter Diego
Velázquez (1599–
1660) portrayed
Saragossa thronged
with visitors.
The Roman bridge
over the Ebro River
can be seen
on the right.

◆**THE MADONNA**
OF THE PILLAR
Goya, c. 1770;
Museo de Bellas
Artes, Saragossa.
Surrounded by
angels, Mary is
shown on the pillar,
holding the baby
Jesus in her arms.
At this early date,
the style of Goya's
work is still relatively
conventional.

◆ **BUILDING**
THE CATHEDRAL
Started in 1681 on a
design by Francisco
Herrera the Younger,
building work on the
cathedral went on
for centuries.
It is a monumental
building and lavishly
decorated. The
interior is 425 x 220
feet (132 x 67 m).

◆**JUAN GOYA WITH**
HIS SON FRANCISCO
Goya's father, an
expert gilder, was
given the task of
checking the quality
of the gilding on all
the sculptures in the
cathedral. At times his
son accompanied him.

GOYA'S LIFE

1. *Francisco was born on March 30, 1746, in the remote village of Fuendetodos. From there he was taken to Saragossa while still a child. His family was of modest status, although his mother was of noble origin. His father was a gilder, a profession which brought the Goya family into contact with artists. During his years at a monastery school Francisco showed an inclination for drawing and an interest in art. At age 13 he entered the workshop of the painter José Luzán Martínez, where he spent much time copying engravings of works by the great masters. Little is known about his youth, but it was almost certainly lively and rich in experiences.* ➤◆

CHARLES III'S MADRID

♦ THE THRONE ROOM
Royal Palace,
Madrid, 1764.
The scaffolding is
being dismantled,
revealing the
spectacular nature
of Tiepolo's ceiling
frescoes.

♦ GIOVANNI BATTISTA
TIEPOLO

Tiepolo was one of the
18th century's most
important artists and
the outstanding
decorative painter of
his time. Born in
Venice in 1696, he
quickly established
a reputation as an
unrivaled interpreter
of myths, allegories,
and stories of Venetian
and European life and
culture. The frescoes
that earned him fame
in Europe for their
elegance and
virtuosity include the
Biblical Stories of the
archbishop's palace
and the decoration of
the cathedral in Udine
(1726–27); *The Course
of the Sun* in the
Palazzo Clerici, Milan
(1740); *Neptune
offering the Riches of
the Sea to Venice* in the
Ducal Palace in Venice
(1748–50); and the
*Homage to the
Emperor Frederick
Barbarossa* (detail
above) in the prince-
bishop's residence in
Würzburg (1752).
When Tiepolo was
summoned to Madrid
by Charles III, he was
elderly though still
prolific. He arrived in
1762, with his sons
and assistants
Domenico and
Lorenzo, and worked
in the Royal Palace,
always highly
honored, until his
death in 1770. His
paintings express a
freedom of execution
and an amazing
feeling for light and
perspective which
certainly influenced
Goya. But in his last
years Tiepolo's
exuberant style was
giving way to the
sober Neoclassicism,
inspired by the ancient
world, that was
establishing itself
in all the arts.

During the late 18th century Spain was passing
through a period of cultural and artistic ferment
as well as political change. King Charles III, while
keeping a firm grip on the reins of power, began
reforming the state apparatus, surrounded himself
with progressive-minded advisers, promoted the arts,
and financed works that glorified the monarchy and
the nation. Madrid was alive with architectural activity.
Many artists and craftsmen were imported from
France, and even more from Italy, to work in the city.
Madrid was adorned with palaces, parks, and avenues,
acquiring the monumental grandeur expected of the
capital of a modern kingdom. Painting was dominated
by Tiepolo, who still worked in the luminous, graceful
Rococo style, and by Mengs, an exponent and theorist
of the rising Neoclassicism. Allegorical paintings of
Spain's history transformed royal rooms and halls into
settings worthy of a glittering court, remote from the
life of the common people.

♦ ANTON MENGS
Self-portrait,
1774; Walker Art
Gallery, Liverpool.
Bohemian by
birth but Roman
by training, Anton

Mengs was appointed
court painter by
Charles III. He
was an excellent
portraitist and helped
Goya launch his
career as an artist.

A MODEL ♦
OF CASERTA
Sabatini, a court
architect, shows a
model of the palace
of the Bourbons at
Caserta in Italy.

Still under
construction at
the time, this vast
palace was a work
by Vanvitelli,
of whom Sabatini
had been a pupil.

♦ **THE BOURBONS AND THE CHURCH**
Members of the Bourbon family occupied several European thrones, including those of Spain and France. In the 18th century, a number of sovereigns were influenced by the rational spirit of the age (often described as the Enlightenment) to introduce reforms. Among them was Charles III of Spain (1716–88), who inherited the throne in 1759, after twenty years as King of Naples, where he had proved himself to be an ardent reformer. Like Naples, Spain was a backward society; after a period of greatness in the 16th century, it had steadily declined. Europe's reforming monarchs tended to see the power of the Catholic Church as an obstacle to progress, and particularly blamed the Jesuit order, which was thought to exercise great covert political influence. Conflict between State and Church culminated in 1767 with the expulsion of the Jesuits from Spain, France, and Naples, and in 1773 the pope was persuaded to suppress the order. Liberals like Goya sympathized with royal policies – until the Bourbons, frightened by the French Revolution, turned to reaction. Above: a satirical etching by Goya, who became more anticlerical over the years: *Against the Common Good*, 1815–20.

♦ **TIEPOLO**
The elderly painter looks proudly at the first of the works commissioned by the Spanish royal family.

♦ **THE KING AND HIS COURTIERS**
Charles III is delighted with the works which are making the Royal Palace in Madrid one of the most sumptuous residences of its time.

2. GOYA'S LIFE ♦ *The young Goya decided to embark on a career as an artist. After his apprenticeship he twice entered the competition for scholarships offered by the Royal Academy of San Fernando in Madrid, but without success. In 1766 he lost to one of his Aragonese contemporaries, Ramón Bayeu, the younger and less talented brother of Francisco Bayeu. The latter had already been acclaimed in Saragossa and at the court of Madrid, where, at only 33, he became the First Painter to the King. In Madrid Goya probably lived with the Bayeu family, and there met Francisco's sister Josefa, who would become his wife. Though Goya's relationship with his illustrious brother-in-law was always difficult, it undoubtedly helped his career.* ⇒

JOURNEY TO ITALY

♦ JOHANN JOACHIM
WINCKELMANN
An archeologist
and art scholar,
Winckelmann was
the leading theorist
of Neoclassicism and
is considered one of
the founders of art
history as a separate
study. Born in
Germany in 1717, he
was fired by a passion
for the classical world.
He studied at the
University of Jena and
in Dresden, and here
he published his
*Thoughts on the
Imitation of Greek Art*,
which greatly
influenced German
artists and thinkers.
He asserted that
classical art should be
observed and imitated
not in order to make
cold copies of it, but
to explore its essence
and spirit and to draw
inspiration from it for
future works.
Winckelmann visited
Italy for the first time
in 1756, settling in
Rome where he met
Mengs. His contact
with the heritage of
ancient Rome, his
admiration for Greek
sculptures studied
from copies made in
the Roman period,
and the discovery of
archeological sites
such as Pompeii and
Herculaneum
provided material for
publications that
have been hugely
influential. The most
important, the *History
of the Art of Antiquity*
(1763), claimed that
Greek and Roman art
represented an ideal
of perfection. This
work could be
considered the
manifesto of
Neoclassicism.
Above: Angelica
Kauffmann,
Winckelmann, 1764;
Kunsthaus, Zurich.

In the 18th century well-born young men were expected
to complete their education with a visit to Italy to admire
the glories of the past. For an artist, such a visit was a
unique opportunity to study masterpieces of many
different periods, from the Greco-Roman world to the
Renaissance, the revolutionary art of Caravaggio, and
the Baroque. Rome more than any other Italian city
embodied this immense cultural heritage, because it was
also the seat of the Papacy. The architecture of Bernini
and Borromini, together with the monuments of
antiquity, gave Rome a grandiose, stagelike appearance.
And it was in Rome that a new artistic style, called
Neoclassicism, emerged, spreading throughout Europe
and, via England, across the ocean to North America.
Exciting archeological discoveries at Herculaneum and
Pompeii around the middle of the century rekindled
enthusiasm for the study of history: as enlightened,
rationalistic theories became established, the past
was explored scientifically and taken as a model for
the new art.

♦ SACRIFICE
TO PRIAPUS
1771; Gudiol
collection, Barcelona.
Like other still rather
schematic works with
classical subjects,
this composition
dates from Goya's
stay in Italy. Goya
painted it so that it
could be sold to pay
his expenses.

3. GOYA'S LIFE ♦ *Around 1770 Goya traveled to Rome,
admiring its architecture and sculpture and discovering
Caravaggio and other great masters of Italian art. During
his stay he took part in a competition held by the Academy
of Parma for a history painting on the subject of the
Carthaginian general Hannibal. The work did not win,
but its expressiveness and grandeur were praised. On his
return to Spain Goya was commissioned to paint a fresco
for the small choir of the chapel of Our Lady of the Pillar in
the cathedral at Saragossa. Within a few months the work
was ready and other commissions for religious paintings
followed. In 1773, Goya married Josefa Bayeu.* ➤

♦ THE APOLLO
BELVEDERE
This statue is a Roman
copy of a Greek bronze
attributed to the
sculptor Leochares,
who lived in the 4th
century B.C. The cult
of Apollo, the god of
light and of beauty,
flourished in ancient
Greece and Rome.

HANNIBAL LOOKS ♦ UPON ITALY FROM THE ALPS
1770–71; private collection. This is the sketch for the painting (now lost) that Goya executed for the competition held by the Academy of Parma in 1771. The work earned a special mention for the artist's fluent brushwork and the grandeur of his conception.

THE CALLING OF ♦ ST. MATTHEW
Caravaggio, 1599–1600; San Luigi dei Francesi, Rome. Of the paintings by Caravaggio (c. 1571–1610) that Goya saw in Rome, the St. Matthew cycle was certainly an important influence on him, with its intense realism, strong contrasts between light and dark, and the dramatic force of the gestures.

♦ THE COURTYARD OF STATUES
Only rich travelers and art scholars were granted the privilege of a nighttime visit to the Octagonal Courtyard inside the Vatican Museums on the hill of the Belvedere.

♦ THE LAOCOÖN
This spectacular marble sculpture from the 1st century B.C. is probably a copy of an older original work. Laocoön, Apollo's priest, and his two sons are crushed by two serpents sent by the goddess Athena. The sculpture was dug up on the Esquiline hill in 1506, and strongly influenced Renaissance artists.

♦ THE FORMER ORANGE GARDEN
The Octagonal Courtyard became the fulcrum of the Vatican Museums, which were created by the 18th-century popes Clement XIV and Pius VI. The reorganization of the space for the exhibition of statues and collections was begun in 1770 and went on until 1796.

JOSEFA BAYEU ♦
A portrait by Goya of his wife, Josefa. The sister of Francisco and Ramón Bayeu, she was known within the family as Pepa. She married Goya in 1773.

♦ **"Lo Spagnuolo" and "il Piazzetta"**
Giuseppe Maria Crespi (1665–1747), though known as "lo Spagnuolo" (the Spaniard), was a Bolognese artist. He drew inspiration from the Carracci, Guido Reni, and 16th-century Venetian painters, and he knew the work of the Flemish and Dutch masters from the Medici collections in Florence. His realism and mastery of chiaroscuro (light and shadow) produced particularly interesting results in religious paintings, which he executed with passionate sincerity.
Above: detail of *The Confirmation* (Gemäldegalerie, Dresden).
His painting greatly influenced another important figure of the time, Giovanni Battista Piazzetta (1683–1754), whose *Ecstasy of St. Francis* is reproduced below. Born in Venice, he founded a painting school in that city, from which the Accademia later developed. He worked in several genres, but was perhaps at his best with religious subjects. His daring perspectives, brilliant colors, and endless imagination made him an outstanding exponent of the decorative art of the late Baroque whose peak was represented by Tiepolo.

Religious Painting

The 18th century was the last period in which religion provided the subjects for a high proportion of the works produced by painters and sculptors. The Old and New Testaments and the lives of the saints and the fathers of the Church offered a huge repertoire of themes and narratives, though usually it was the patron who decided what the subject should be. Religious authorities commissioned their chosen artist to execute a work on a given subject, reserving the right to approve the sketches and cartoons. Nobles and princes often ordered pious works for churches or private chapels. In Spain, patronage for secular purposes was rare outside Madrid, and so Goya began his career as a painter of religious works. These earned him the money and prestige he needed to establish himself.

♦ **The Adoration of the Name of God by Angels**
Though destined for the *coreto*, the small choir of a chapel in Saragossa's cathedral of El Pilar, this fresco is of a considerable size: 23 x 49 feet (7 x 15 m). It was the first major commission executed by Goya, who drew inspiration for it from the Italian Baroque. He received 15,000 reals for it – a large sum for an artist making his debut.

Details ♦
Imposing forms and colors shot through with light: Goya has assimilated Tiepolo's lesson. Although not reaching the sublime heights of the Italian master, he showed great promise in this first commission. The two details are from the final sketch, 1772; Gudiol, Barcelona.

♦ THE DREAM
OF JOSEPH
1771; Museo de
Bellas Artes,
Saragossa.
This work belongs to
a cycle of paintings
executed by Goya in
1771 for the chapel of
the Sobradiel Palace
in Saragossa.
The work reveals a
considerable mastery
of composition and
of the treatment of
light and forms.
The angel is arranged
as a series of curved
lines, which
accentuate its
softness.

♦ THE CIRCUMCISION
1774; detail. This is
one of the *Scenes from
the Life of the Virgin*
for the chapel of the
Aula Dei monastery.
The colors have not
been applied evenly,
but are free and often
interrupted, with
visible brushstrokes,
decidedly an
innovation as far
as Spanish art
was concerned.
The simple figures,
almost lacking in
any detail, are
solemn and
impressive.

4. GOYA'S LIFE ♦ *An important commission, obtained
with Bayeu's help, was for a great cycle of frescoes in the
chapel of the Charterhouse of Aula Dei, a few miles from
Saragossa. In less than a year Goya finished eleven
compositions, which represent the culmination of his
early work. By this time Goya was expressing himself
with great technical assurance and was beginning to
develop a highly personal style. No doubt his ambition
was to conquer the capital and the court. And in fact in
1744 he was called to Madrid by the painter Mengs, who
managed the royal tapestry works of Santa Barbara.
Soon he would become a fashionable painter.* ➡♦

♦ THE BURIAL OF
CHRIST
1771; Lázaro Galdiano
Museum, Madrid.
Goya studied and
practiced his art with
passion, and very
quickly achieved a
remarkable technical
confidence. His
personality is not
yet apparent in this
youthful work, which
nonetheless shows
his skill in creating
solemn, monumental
forms and in using
light. The composition
was copied from an
engraving by the
French painter Simon
Vouet (1641), which
Goya had seen in
Luzán's workshop.

GOYA'S MASTERS

By about 1780 the artistic climate at the court of Charles III had changed. Mengs was the last influential foreign painter to be employed, and from this time onward it was Spanish artists who contended for the favors of official patrons, the benevolence of the royal family, and the highest positions in the academic hierarchy. The palaces of the royal family and the aristocracy contained many examples of the art of the past, above all the masterpieces of the 17th-century *siglo de oro*, the golden age of Spanish art. During this period the influence of Italian artists, particularly Caravaggio, led to the creation of a realistic school whose masters were José de Ribera, active in Naples, and Diego Velázquez. In Velázquez, whose works he had copied as a boy, Goya discovered the magic of atmosphere. From the Dutch painter Rembrandt he learned how to use light. Later he would say, "I have had three masters, Rembrandt, Velázquez, and nature."

♦ **REMBRANDT**
Rembrandt (1606–69) was one of the supreme geniuses of art. He was born and died in Holland, produced a large number of paintings and engravings, and had many followers and imitators.
The essence of his art was light. Departing from the most literal type of realism, Rembrandt arrived at a transfiguration of reality through the use of light, producing effects of incredible intensity and dramatic force, as in *The Night Watch* (detail below) of 1642 (Rijksmuseum, Amsterdam), or in the *Self-Portrait* of 1660 (above) in the Louvre, one of his last masterpieces.
Goya himself named Rembrandt as one of his masters. Rembrandt's influence is particularly apparent in Goya's night scenes, and in his treatment of darkness and shadow, for instance in the portrait of *The Family of the Infante Don Luis*.
Rembrandt's mastery as a painter was at least equaled by his mastery as an engraver. The same could be said of Goya, who applied himself to this technique with results of the highest level.

♦ **HIS FIRST MASTER**
Luzán, *Appearance of the Virgin of El Pilar*, 1764; Our Lady of Cogulada, Saragossa. The thirteen-year-old

Goya executed his early works in the workshop of Luzán, a good teacher and modestly gifted painter who had studied in Italy.

♦ **THE ADORATION OF THE NAME OF GOD**
Giaquinto, 1741–43; Santa Croce in Jerusalem, Rome. This distinguished Italian painter in the pure Rococo style was a pupil of Luca Giordano in Naples. He came to Spain in 1752 and frescoed one of the chapels in the cathedral of El Pilar in Saragossa. Here Goya could admire his fine colors and airy, graceful compositions, which seemed refreshingly new in the context of contemporary Aragonese art.

5. GOYA'S LIFE ♦ *In 1775 Goya settled in Madrid and started to correspond with his friend Martín Zapater. He wrote about his work, but also about his debts, his patron, the minister Floridablanca, his passion for hunting, and his taste for chocolate. He executed the cartoons for the tapestries that were to be hung in the dining room of the Prince of the Asturias, the heir to the Spanish throne. These splendid works portrayed scenes of popular life which were much admired by the princess María Luisa. In the royal collections Goya discovered the art of Velázquez and, from 1756 to 1778, he engraved the works of this artist, whom he recognized as his master.* ➤

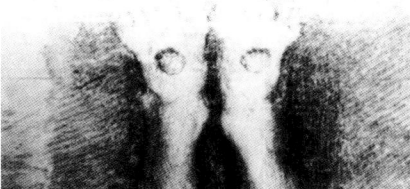

◆ MENGS

Christ on the Cross, 1761–69, Prado, Madrid. (The details are from a preparatory sketch.) This is a very different interpretation of the suffering of Christ. The tension of the anatomically well-defined body is combined with the artist's interest in the details of the scene (the plaque on the cross, the skull at its base) and in the background of colored light. This is one of Mengs's best works. Although far from the naturalism of Velázquez, it has its own majesty and force.

◆ GOYA

Christ on the Cross, 1780, Prado, Madrid. Goya presented this work at the examination for admission to the Academy of San Fernando. While the dark background and coloring were inspired by Velázquez's painting, the work also shows the influence of Mengs, probably because a fairly conventional piece would ensure election to the Academy. Goya painted a classical body, concentrating all the dramatic force in the upturned face.

◆ VELÁZQUEZ

Crucified Christ, 1631, Prado, Madrid. The human drama of the crucifixion is rendered by the use of chiaroscuro, indistinct outlines, and rapid brush-strokes, suggesting the solidity of the reclining head contributes to the work's expressive force. Goya was awestruck by the atmosphere created. He assimilated much that Velázquez had to teach, and felt especially close to him.

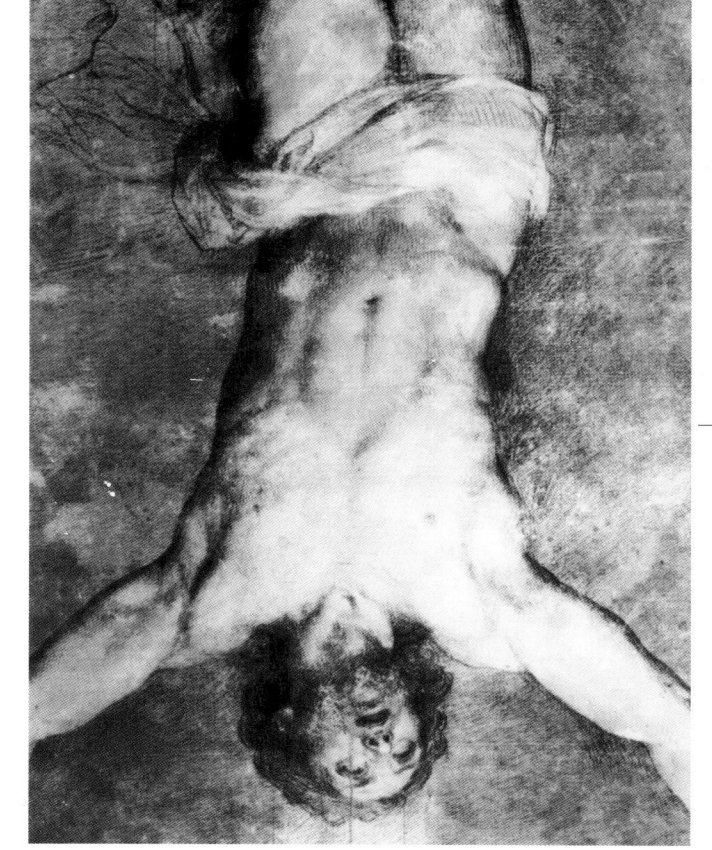

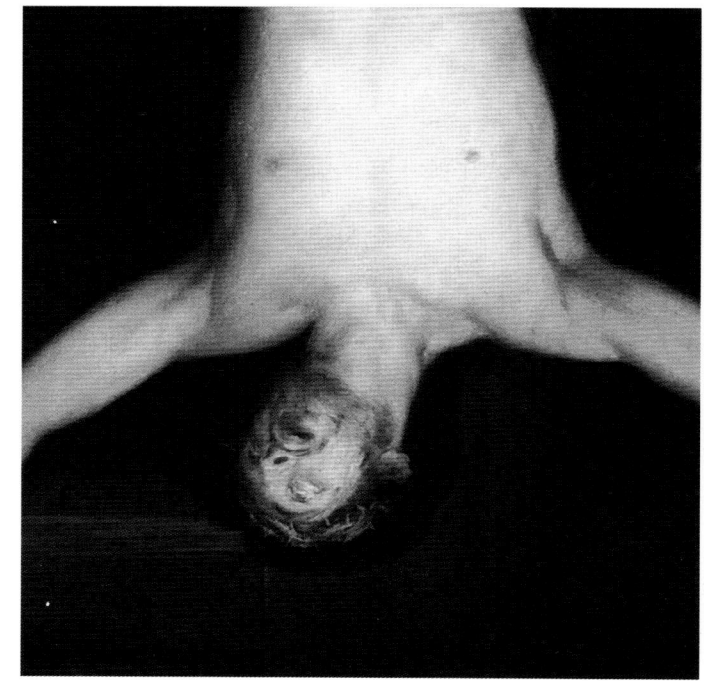

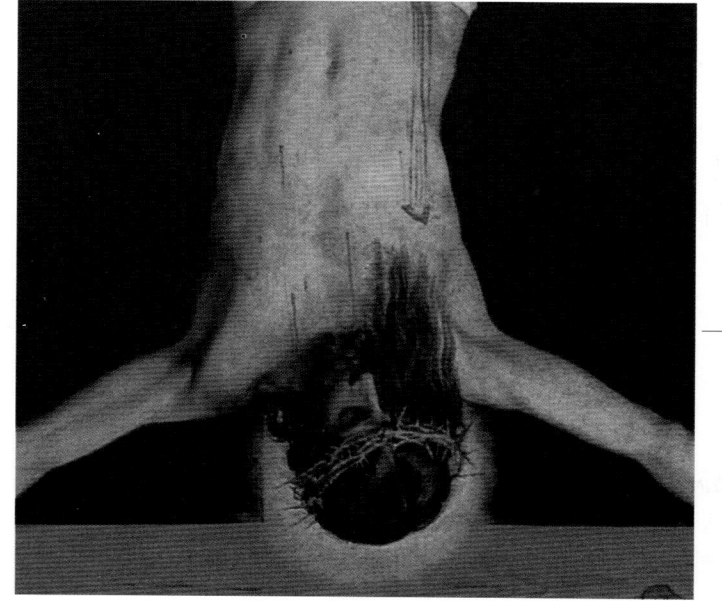

◆ VELÁZQUEZ

Diego Velázquez (1599–1660) was born in Seville. In his early works he was inspired by the realism of Caravaggio and his Neapolitan followers, who were well known in Velázquez's native city. In 1623 he became court painter to Philip IV and settled in Madrid, where he studied the works of Titian and Rubens in the royal collections.

A journey to Italy took him to Genoa, Milan, Venice, Parma, Rome, and Naples, where he became acquainted with the great artists of his time.

His remarkable skills as a colorist, which brought him close to the Venetian tradition, became particularly evident on his return to Madrid where he executed a splendid series of works. His portraits did not idealize the sitters, but instead remained close to the psychological truth about them. His historical subjects became scenes of everyday life, and his landscapes were imbued with subtle nuances and great vibrancy. Velázquez's art was characterized by an exploration into the possibilities of light and by a technical and compositional freedom which represented a break with tradition and heralded the art of Goya and the 19th century. Because of this Velázquez was not fully understood in his own time.

Above: *The Clown Sebastián de Morra*, c. 1644, Prado, Madrid.

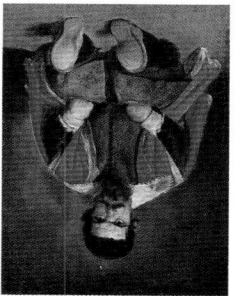

THE ROYAL TAPESTRY WORKS

The custom of covering walls with tapestries, that is, with specially woven fabric pictures, had a practical as well as a decorative purpose. Lining a room with fabrics meant protecting it from cold and drafts. The tradition of tapestry-weaving goes back centuries. In the 14th century it spread into France and became even more important as a major industry in Flanders. In fact, the word "arras," often used for a tapestry, comes from the name of the city of Arras, a great manufacturing center. In the 16th century tapestry works were founded in Italy; the cartoons were supplied by artists such as Raphael. The art of tapestry-making then developed in several stylistic directions. To serve the court of the Spanish Bourbons in Madrid, the Royal Tapestry Works of Santa Barbara was founded under the direction of Francisco Van der Goten, the son of a Flemish tapestry-weaver, Jacob, who settled in Spain in 1720. The royal tapestries were of excellent workmanship, with hunting scenes and landscapes as the subjects most favored.

♦ **THE CROCKERY VENDOR**
1778; Prado, Madrid. The people in Goya's cartoons were almost always common folk, portrayed in pleasant and lively situations. Such scenes gave a misleadingly idyllic picture of the world, in which it suited the royal family to believe; yet Goya succeeded in imbuing them with an astonishing vitality.

♦ **THE ROYAL WEAVERS**
In the Tapestry Works of Santa Barbara workers weave the tapestries from behind, using the threads on the loom to reproduce the cartoon supplied by the artist. The woolen threads in a wide range of colors and shades are wound around long wooden bobbins.

♦ **THE LOOMS**
Tapestries may be woven on either vertical or horizontal looms. On a vertical loom the tapestry-worker moves the threads on the loom manually. On a horizontal loom the threads are moved by means of pedals.

THE SPINNING MILL ♦
At the Tapestry Works spinners prepare the wools, winding them on long wooden bobbins. A wide range of colors ensures a realistic effect in the reproduction of the scenes portrayed.

♦ THE PARASOL
1777; Prado, Madrid. This is the most famous of Goya's 63 tapestry cartoons. As the tapestry was to be hung above the door in the dining room of the Prince of the Asturias, the figures are shown as if from below. Dazzling with color, the cartoon shows a fine mastery of brushwork.

♦ VELAZQUEZ'S SPINNERS
1657; Prado, Madrid. Tapestry-weavers came to Spain from France and Flanders from the 14th century. As this painting shows, by the 17th century there was a workshop in Madrid where tapestries were repaired. Keeping tapestries in good condition was not easy, and they had to be washed periodically to preserve them from moths.

♦ VAN DER GOTEN
Francisco Van der Goten directed the Tapestry Works of Santa Barbara with the help of his father Jacob, who was the most prestigious figure in the tapestry-making industry. When Jacob moved to Spain he brought with him the secrets of his craft.

6. GOYA'S LIFE ♦ *Six of Goya's children were born between 1775 and 1784, but four died in infancy and only the last, Javier, outlived his father. The artist Mengs died in 1779. Goya applied for his seat in the Academy of San Fernando and was unanimously elected in 1780. But in the same year he was humiliated after the chapter of the cathedral of El Pilar in Saragossa commissioned him to fresco the dome of the Chapel of St. Joachim. His work was criticized by his brother-in-law Francicso Bayeu, the chapter agreed, and Goya was forced to "correct" the frescoes. Soon afterward, a royal commission to decorate San Francisco el Grande in Madrid restored his self-esteem.* ➸

THE MEADOW OF ST. ISIDORE

♦ THE WORK
The Meadow of St. Isidore, 1788; oil on canvas, 17 x 37 inches (44 x 94 cm); Prado, Madrid.
The work is one of five preliminary sketches for a cartoon for a tapestry intended for the children's bedchamber in the Pardo Palace. Goya wrote about it to Martín Zapater on May 31, 1788 : "I am hard at work on it and with some tension because there is little time and because it is something that the sovereigns will see."

Goya was in fact unenthusiastic about the commission, but as a painter paid by the king he could hardly refuse it. The rich detail, the number of figures, and the subtle treatment of the pictorial space would have presented serious problems for the tapestry-weavers, but in the end the tapestry was never made. All five sketches were presented to the king in the summer of 1789 and the final composition was then started, but the series was interrupted because of the death of Charles III. Later Goya sold the work to the Duke of Osuna. Between 1820 and 1823 Goya painted *Pilgrimage of St. Isidore*, a very different, macabre piece evoking mystery and evil. The two paintings epitomize the development of his vision as a man and artist.
Above: *The Hermitage of St. Isidore*, 1788; Prado, Madrid.

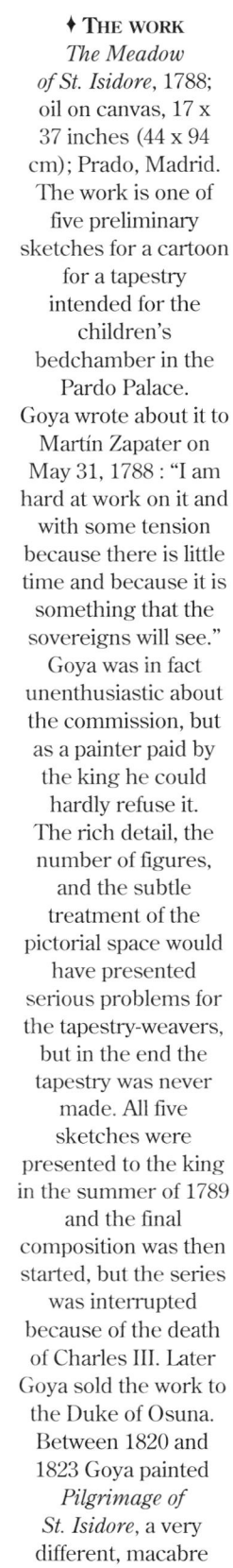

It is a beautiful day in mid-May, spring is in the air, and the afternoon sky is tinged with pink. People gather on the banks of the Manzanares for the feast of St. Isidore, the patron saint of Madrid. The background displays a panorama of the city, dominated by the monumental forms of the Palacio Real (the Royal Palace) and the church of San Francisco. In the foreground are horses, carts, carriages, and vast crowds of people. Common folk and elegant ladies, boys and horsemen talking, drinking, looking, and being looked at .... Goya seems to be there too, trying to capture the air, the light, the movement, to paint from real life – as his friend Zapater wrote a few days later – the crowd with its myriad colors, to set down on canvas the atmosphere of a religious occasion that is also a holiday gathering, a real festival of the people.

♦ THE BACKGROUND Standing out in the hazy light are Madrid's monumental palaces, which form the background of the painting. Because of the vastness of the horizon they play a very important part in the composition of the picture.

This charming, happy work is a hymn to the joy of life, and an unwitting tribute to a period in history that was about to end. The century of the Enlightenment was drawing to a close and the Spanish monarchy was on the eve of a crisis. But today is the day of St. Isidore and the world is still golden and alive with beauty and pleasure.

Goya's vibrant colors and his pictorial technique, involving small touches of the brush, are a foretaste of the treatment of everyday scenes in 19th-century painting.

♦ THE "MAJAS"
Dressed in white, fresh, and graceful under their parasols, pretty maidens are courted by elegant young men. Goya's brushstrokes are rapid and assured and his pictorial technique heralds that of 19th-century French painters such as Gustave Courbet.

♦ CARTS AND CROWDS
A few brushstrokes, barely sketched figures, a scene brimming with movement and life, like a snapshot. We can almost hear the hubbub of voices and noises rising from the meadow where the crowd has gathered.

♦ THE PILGRIMAGE OF ST. ISIDORE
1821–23;
Prado, Madrid.
This dark, desperate painting was executed well over 30 years after the radiant *Meadow of St. Isidore*. A procession of believers, their mouths gaping in hysterical credulity, moves toward the shrine of the saint on the hill. The work is characterized by its eerily dark tones, and, in fact, belongs to the group of "black paintings" done by Goya directly onto the walls of his house during one of the most troubled periods of his life. The complete painting is reproduced below. Two details are also shown.

THE ACADEMY

The word "academy" comes from Greek and was originally the name of the place where the philosopher Plato conversed with his disciples. The first art academies appeared in Italy in the late 16th century under the impulse of the neo-Platonic literary, philosophic, and scientific movement begun by Marsilio Ficino at the Medici court in Florence. Academies differed from guilds in that they conferred a social status on artists which was distinct from that of craftsmen. In the 17th century, art academies multiplied in Europe, working to maintain artistic standards but also tending to become conservative bodies, hostile to innovation. For centuries the workshop had been the only place where a person could learn to be an artist; but toward the end of the 18th century art became a subject that was taught in schools or academies, involving copying and drawing from real life, and lessons in anatomy, geometry, and perspective.

♦ THE ALTARPIECE
The king, through his chief minister, the Count of Floridablanca, ordered the decoration of the church of San Francisco el Grande, holding a competition in which the most distinguished painters at court took part. Goya wrote: "And finally ... it seemed that God remembered me." The competition was in fact a great opportunity for him to measure himself against members of the Academy who were older and better established than he was. Goya, Bayeu, and Maella received commissions, and Goya's work, executed between 1781 and 1784, was very well received. This in large part compensated him for Bayeu's humiliation of him during the decoration of the St. Joachim Chapel in the cathedral of El Pilar in Saragossa. Nowadays art critics tend to disagree with the verdict of the judges: the work is held to be static and stereotyped, and certainly not among Goya's best. We may see it as evidence of the artist's self-confidence in accommodating himself to the standards laid down by the Academy. In the altarpiece (right), note the interesting portraits of the figures surrounding the saint, particularly that of Goya himself, seen on the right (detail above). Goya was 35 years old at this time.

♦ THE PRESENTATION
July 5, 1780: Goya presents his *Christ on the Cross* to members of the Academy of San Fernando. His admission to the Academy, an event necessary for the advancement of his career, depends on their judgment.

THE DEBATE ♦
Members of the Academy unanimously approve the work. They discuss its technique, correctness, plasticity, and the dignity with which the sacred subject is rendered.

♦ ST. BERNARDINE OF SIENA PREACHING TO KING ALFONSO V
1781; San Francisco el Grande, Madrid. Goya's altarpiece met the Academy's standards.

MARIANO ♦ SALVADOR MAELLA
Maella had been the follower of Giaquinto in Rome, and after the death of Mengs had replaced the German artist as Court Painter.

20

♦ GOYA HUMBLED
Goya's fresco *Mary, Queen of Martyrs* for El Pilar was executed in nine months. This was very swift by the standards of Bayeu, who supervised the work; he ordered Goya to change it, demanding that the work be given a more "finished" appearance, closer to the academic perfection that was so unlike the freedom of Goya's style.

♦ THE KITE
1778; Prado, Madrid. This tapestry cartoon by Goya, with its lively subject, is comparable in its atmosphere to *The Parasol* (page 17). A group of young men are enjoying the sight of their kite flying against a sunset-lit sky.

♦ NUDE LESSON
A compulsory subject for painters and sculptors was the study of real-life nudes.

Pupils had to copy the models and practice sketching figures while studying the intricacies of human anatomy.

♦ BAYEU BROTHERS
Francisco and Ramón Bayeu, Goya's brothers-in-law, were members of the Academy. Francisco, nicknamed Bayeu the Great, was regarded as the best Spanish painter at the court of Charles III.

7. GOYA'S LIFE ♦ *The years after 1780 were marked by great successes, including a series of magnificent portraits. Enlightened intellectuals such as Jovellanos and powerful reforming ministers like Floridablanca and other influential figures at court admired Goya, posed for him, and became his personal friends. Goya did a great deal of work for the king and the royal princes, especially for the Marquis of Pañafiel and his wife, the future Duke and Duchess of Osuna. In 1784 he portrayed the entire family of Don Luis, Charles III's younger brother. In 1786 he was appointed Court Painter. A year later he may have visited Paris: he certainly studied French.* ➡

THE ENLIGHTENED DESPOTS

In the 18th century a number of European rulers sought to legitimize their absolute power, not as monarchs by divine right, but as progressive-minded guardians of the state. These "Enlightened Despots" favored educational, economic, scientific, and technical reform, and the suppression of traditional privileges, including the privileges of the Church. In Spain the desire for reform was embodied by Charles III in the period 1770–78 and by intellectuals such as Jovellanos, but it was held back by the lack of a substantial middle class. The most urgent problem was the inadequacy of agriculture in the south, where the population was rising fast. Charles's policies aimed to improve communications (canals and roads), suppress ecclesiastical privileges, and increase agricultural production by way of new farming methods.

♦ **FREDERICK II OF PRUSSIA** (1712–86) After a strict military upbringing, but also a modern intellectual education on the French model, Frederick came to the throne in 1740. The prototype of an Enlightened Despot, he quickly affirmed the importance of his role as a ruler who should be the "first servant of the state," as he wrote in his *Antimachiavel* (1739). From Rheinsberg castle, where he dedicated himself to his studies and to the arts in order to complete his education (1735–40), he engaged in a voluminous correspondence with the great writers of his time, including Voltaire, whose advice he often welcomed. He was responsible for legislative reforms and for the recruitment of an official class that would help make Prussia a great power in the next decades. A military genius, Frederick reorganized the army and proved able to fight off the numerically superior forces of Austria, Russia, and France in the Seven Years' War (1756–63). His reforms included the suppression of torture, the proclamation of the freedom of religion and opinion, and measures aimed at improving agriculture and industry. In 1763 he promulgated regulations making primary education compulsory. Above: Frederick II and Voltaire.

♦ **CHARLES III IN THE GUISE OF A HUNTER** 1786–88; private collection, Madrid. Charles reigned from 1759 to 1788, surrounded by an intellectual elite bent on turning Spain into a modern state. Here Goya portrayed him dressed as a huntsman. The artist certainly had in mind his master Velázquez, who was also an accomplished royal portraitist.

♦ **THE COURT OF FLORIDABLANCA** (1728–1808) One of the greatest of reform-minded Spaniards, Floridablanca began his career as a jurist, then became ambassador in Italy, and finally chief minister as Secretary of State (1777). Goya admired his ideas and so he was particularly proud to receive the commission for this official portrait. *José Moñino, Count of Floridablanca, with Goya and the Architect Sabatini*, 1783; Banco Urquijo, Madrid.

♦ **THE FOUR CROPS** Cultivated in rotation, the crops are (in a clockwise direction): wheat (exploitation of the soil), clover (pasturage for animals without impoverishing the soil), barley (exploitation), and turnips (renewal).

8. GOYA'S LIFE ♦ *In January 1789 Charles IV came to the throne. Goya was asked to paint portraits of the king and queen for the coronation and was appointed Court Painter. In this period he was experimenting with new artistic techniques. News of the French Revolution disturbed life at the court, where Goya's liberal protectors were soon in a critical position. Floridablanca was removed and Goya himself experienced some difficulties. In 1790 the king commissioned a new series of tapestry cartoons. Goya was unwilling to go on with this kind of work but dared not refuse the king's order. He subsequently asked for leave and spent time first in Valencia, then in Andalusia.* ➤

♦ **AGRICULTURAL DEVELOPMENT**
The development of agriculture was linked to the increase in population which began in Europe in the 16th century and took off in the 18th. It was particularly important in England, where new farming methods and machines were introduced by enterprising landowners.The four-year Norfolk crop rotation gets its name from the region where it was first tried out by Charles "Turnip" Townshend (1674–1738).

♦ **RENEWAL**
The cultivation of turnips, corn, potatoes, hemp, or tomatoes enriches the soil, which no longer needs to lie fallow between cycles of cereals.

CANALS ♦
Building canals guaranteed higher yields. This was one of the common factors in the economic policies of the sovereigns of the Enlightenment.

COUNT FRANCISCO ♦ **CABARRUS**
1786–87; Banco de España, Madrid. A leading banker and economist, Cabarrús belonged to the group of reformers who sought to shake Spain out of its torpor. He founded the National Bank and enjoyed great political influence until the antiliberal reaction set in.

♦ **CATHERINE II AND MAXIMILIAN FRANZ**
Catherine II, tsarina of Russia, seized power with a coup d'état in 1762. She confiscated property from the Orthodox Church in order to improve state finances and create institutions of higher education. She favored free primary schooling and was an admirer of Voltaire and Diderot, with whom she corresponded, purchasing their libraries in order to stimulate a Russian cultural revival. However, the enlightened schemes she propounded tended to remain on paper rather than being put into practice, and after the French Revolution her views became reactionary. A commission entrusted with the task of legislative reform worked for eleven years from 1767 but failed to resolve the central problem of serfdom. During the same period Maximilian Franz (1756–1801), the prince-bishop of Bonn, brother of the emperor Joseph II, promoted enlightened ideas in his small principality within the Holy Roman Empire. He reformed the judiciary, abolished torture, and reduced the privileges of the nobility. His great cultural initiatives included the opening of a public reading room in the palatine library and the foundation of Bonn University. Above: a portrait by Lampi, 1794.

♦ **POPULATION GROWTH**
In many European areas the population continued to grow throughout the century, making necessary a more rational use of resources.

23

THE FAMILY OF THE INFANTE DON LUIS

A moment of togetherness in an interior scene. Evening has fallen and the room is enveloped in darkness. We are in the residence of the king's younger brother, Don Luis, who seems to have been distracted from a game of cards. Behind him are two of his children, while his pretty young wife is having her hair combed by a servant. Their younger daughter is held in the arms of a wet nurse. On the left, with the children, are two female servants and, in the foreground, Goya at his easel, but turned toward his sitters. On the right stand a well-dressed gentleman, two servants, and another outsider, possibly a groom or coachman, with a surprisingly bold, vivid smile. Fourteen figures make a masterpiece in which realism and poetry, affection and sincerity are combined. There is nothing official, pompous, or academic here, but instead an extraordinary immediacy, an authentic innovation in the history of painting.

♦ **THE WORK**
The Family of the Infante Don Luis, oil on canvas, 98 x 130 inches (248 x 330 cm); Magnani Rocca Foundation, Corte di Mamiano, Parma. The work was executed during Goya's stay in the residence at Arenas de San Pedro near Avila, where the king's brother had retired with his morganatic wife, María Teresa de Vallabriga, and the children born from a union that had violated dynastic rules. The young woman was the daughter of a cavalry captain and, not being of noble blood, could not marry an infante of Spain and hope to have her children recognized as of royal status. Originally destined for the Church, Don Luis was thirty years older than his wife. A collector and art connoisseur, he shared with Goya a passion for hunting. Relations between the two men were very friendly and this probably encouraged the idea of painting an intimate group portrait. Remarkably, until 1967 this painting was known only through a small copy and had never been exhibited to the public. It had been kept in seclusion in Florence, where its owners were the Ruspoli family, who had inherited it at the beginning of the century. Since 1974 it has belonged to the Magnani Rocca Foundation and it is of course fully accessible.

♦ **THE LITTLE MARIA TERESA**
The elder daughter of Don Luis and María Teresa de Vallabriga is three or four years old. Goya portrays her prettily sharp-eyed as she turns inquisitively toward him.

♦ **A SPANISH FACE**
Although the identity of this person is not known, the face is unforgettable for its frank smile and the directness of its gaze.

In this painting we see that Goya has assimilated the lessons of Caravaggio and Rembrandt. The light is the key element. From out of the darkness only the mistress of the house emerges fully: the candle illuminates her, highlighting her white nightgown. She is the central figure of the painting and also of the family. Goya has achieved an impressive compositional unity, concentrating the light in the center and carefully observing the play of its reflections on the faces, fabrics, and clothes. He has removed all furnishings and needless details and has concentrated on the essential in order to lend greater emphasis to the expressions of the protagonists, their characters, and the relationships that link them. Unexpectedly, we notice that princes and servants have the same dignity. For this reason too, the painting is a significant innovation.

Goya, 1800; De
Sueca, Madrid.
Here is María Teresa
(the girl on the left in
the painting of the
family of Don Luis),
now grown into the
unhappy wife of a
court favorite, Godoy.
In this portrait, Goya
is affectionately on
the side of the
countess.

THE PROTAGONIST ♦
In the center of
Velázquez's painting
is the five-year-old
blonde Infanta of
Spain. She has a
childlike grace but
also a self-assured
awareness of
her own role.

THE MENINAS ♦
Diego Velázquez,
1656; Prado, Madrid.
This is one of the
most celebrated
works in all Spanish
art. Its subject is the
five-year-old Infanta
Margherita and

her maidservants.
The painter is shown
standing on the left,
in front of his canvas.
The viewpoint is
that of the king and
queen, whose images
are reflected in
the mirror.

♦A SERVANT
The painting has two
titles, *Las Meninas*
(The Maidservants)
and *The Family of
Philip IV*. In this detail
the intense little face
of one of the maid-

servants is illuminated
by a ray of light from
the side. The work is
an intricate play of
cross-references, as
the nine figures, on
various levels, are
gradually revealed.

COURT PAINTER

Painting at the king's command, coming to know the royal family, immortalizing it on canvas, and being well paid for his trouble: this was the life that Goya enjoyed as a Court Painter, an official position that can be compared to the present-day role of a celebrity's "personal photographer." In 1789 Goya had written enthusiastically about the princes of the Asturias, his future sovereigns: "I have kissed their hands: never until now have I had such good fortune." Now he had succeeded in winning a leading position, the queen's sympathy, and the esteem of the king and the court. But the more Goya became familiar with court life and, in particular, with the king's immediate circle, the more clearly he saw what lay behind the gold and the luxury: caprice, corruption, self-indulgence, and deceit. He became disenchanted, and the more or less overt adulation of royalty which his duties involved weighed heavily on him. As an artist he wanted to be a free man, not a courtier.

♦ INTELLECTUAL FRIENDS
Goya's artistic talent, along with his passionate curiosity and his continual desire to learn, brought him into contact with an advanced intellectual environment that was very different from the intrigue- and gossip-ridden court.
He associated with historians, thinkers, writers, and economists, who discussed intellectual matters and the problems of the society in which they lived.
With men like Cabarrús, Saavedra, Melendes Valdés, and De Iriarte, Goya learned about the evil conditions in Spain, its isolation, and the backwardness that led to widespread superstition and prejudice. To such men, injustice and abuses of power seemed anachronistic when Europe was seething with new ideas. Among the more liberal and enlightened Spanish intellectuals with whom Goya became friends, Melchor de Jovellanos (1744– 1811) was particularly active in influencing him and helping him.
It was Jovellanos who, in 1798, obtained for him a commission to fresco the dome of San Antonio de la Florida.
Goya portrayed Jovellanos standing cross-legged, in the English style.
This was no accident: England was a model of tolerance and culture admired by reformers. Above: portrait of Jovellanos, 1785; Valls y Taberner, Madrid.

♦ THE ESCORIAL
The immense, austere palace, situated near Madrid in the foothills of the Sierra de Guadarrama, was built for Philip II, who conceived of it as a monastic city and mausoleum of the Habsburg dynasty. Charles IV's family resided there during the summer months.

9. GOYA'S LIFE ♦ *Late in 1792, Goya began to suffer from a serious illness which for six months had him fighting for his life. A relapse resulted in permanent deafness, and he was unable to work until the summer of 1793. Meanwhile the young and handsome Godoy had become supreme; favored by Queen María Luisa, he was given the title Prince of the Peace. Court life was becoming more reactionary and treacherous and the Inquisition returned to terrorize intellectual dissenters. However, Goya's health improved and he returned to Madrid in 1793; he had changed, even spiritually, though he retained his official position.* ≫↓

♦ PORTRAIT OF THE QUEEN
Goya paints a portrait of María Luisa of Bourbon in the Escorial palace. An entire team of hairdressers, tailors, and maidservants are at the service of the queen, who must look her best for the portrait.

MARIA LUISA ♦
The queen was strong-willed, an intriguer, ambitious, and extravagant. It was said that she was the real king of Spain. since Charles IV was weak, indolent, and not very intelligent.

♦ MANUEL GODOY
The queen's lover was a handsome, cynical, pleasure-loving man. He was hated by the people, but had great power at court. He was made prime minister in 1792, when he was still only twenty-five, and was later created Prince of the Peace.

♦ STANDING SELF-PORTRAIT
1793–95; private collection, Madrid. Goya painted numerous self-portraits. In this one he shows himself robust in stature, with marked features. His expression is of intense concentration as he works at his easel. Candles fixed in his hat provide the light he needs.

A HORSE ✦ CALLED MARCIAL
This splendid animal, a gift from Godoy to the queen, was equipped with saddle-cloths and festive decorations for the portrait.

✦ MARIA LUISA ON HORSEBACK
1799; Prado, Madrid. This work, which greatly pleased the queen, thanks to its faithful rendering of the subjects (even the horse!), is remarkable for its naturalness. María Luisa looks amused, assured, and almost triumphant.

GOYA AT WORK ✦
Goya was very quick to capture the features of his models. Three sittings were usually enough. Here he asks the queen to be patient and to hold her pose.

CHARLES IV ✦ ON HORSEBACK
1799; Prado, Madrid. Equestrian portraits dignified their subjects and so were highly valued. Those painted by Goya were very forceful and reveal the artist's insight into the subject's personality.

LOS CAPRICHOS

In his early fifties, Goya was driven to experiment with new means of expression, entering a prolific creative phase. In 1797–98 he executed small paintings on metal, recording highly personal sensations and states of mind, full of imagination, which he could not express in his official works. He produced paintings about witch-craft and superstition, but a series of 80 etchings called *Los Caprichos* ("The Caprices") released his most ironic vein and unleashed the monsters and obsessions that lurked in his mind. Mixing satire with fantasy, Goya's work seemed too provocative to tolerate, and the Inquisition suppressed the *Caprichos*. Goya was indeed critical of the social and religious order. But today the *Caprichos* are seen as going beyond satire to draw upon the unconscious, bringing into play forces that would not be recognized and analyzed for another century.

♦ **FUSELI: THE NIGHTMARE**
1781; Bibliothèque Nationale, Paris. Goya was a close contemporary of Johann Heinrich Füssli (1741–1825), a Swiss-born painter who worked mainly in England and became known as Henry Fuseli. Like Goya, Fuseli was not entirely at home in the calm, rational atmosphere of the Enlightenment and Neoclassicism. He showed an early enthusiasm for the classical world extolled by Winckelmann, but also responded to the "terribleness" of Michelangelo's art, which he felt mirrored his own restless temperament. His haunted and fantastic images place him among the forerunners of Romantic art. Like Goya in *The Sleep of Reason Produces Monsters*, Fuseli saw in sleep the loss of reason, which he symbolized in *The Nightmare* (above) by surrounding the sleeping woman with strange, obsessive figures. Fuseli's innovative painting attracted attention all over Europe. We do not know whether Goya saw it. As well as the original painting, Fuseli made an engraved version. The technique Goya used was that of etching combined with aquatint. This produced splendid chiaroscuro effects, and made the figures stand out against the background, giving a rather sinister impact.

GOD FORGIVE HER, ♦ SHE WAS HER MOTHER
The title of each etching in the series is a characteristic phrase whose meaning, some two centuries later, is not always clear. Here the artist denounces his contemporaries' backwardness and openness to bribery.

♦ **THE SLEEP OF REASON PRODUCES MONSTERS**
This is the most celebrated of the *Caprichos*, and was intended to be the frontispiece of the series. Bats and other nocturnal creatures surround the sleeping man, whose mind is not controlled by his reason.

10. GOYA'S LIFE ♦ *Recovered from his illness, Goya resumed work. In addition to official commissions, he devoted himself to a freer kind of painting consisting of "inventions and caprices." In 1795 he executed portraits of Francisco Bayeu (who died that same year) and the Duke and Duchess of Alba. He was appointed Director of Painting at the Academy, and he became a close friend of the Alba family. After a visit to Andalusia and Seville, he stayed with the Duchess of Alba, now a widow, in her residence at Sanlúcar. Here Goya spent some peaceful but also very fruitful months in the company of the duchess, whom he portrayed several times.* ⟫♦

Copies of *Los Caprichos* were put on sale in the workshop of a liquor and perfume seller in the Calle Desengaño, Madrid. In February 1799, about twenty days after their publication, the etchings were confiscated.

♦ **THEY ALREADY HAVE A SEAT**
Stupidity and ignorance are symbolized by two girls who, determined to be fashionable, wear ludicrously short petticoats and put chairs on their heads. The Spanish word *asientos* means both "chairs" and "common sense."

♦ **SEVEN COPIES SOLD**
Of the seven sets of etchings sold before their confiscation, five were bought by the Duke and Duchess of Osuna, patrons of Goya.

♦ **GOYA: THE WITCHES' SABBATH**
1797–98; Lázaro Galdiano Museum, Madrid. This work belongs to the same period as *Los Caprichos* and its fantastic vision is similarly grotesque and destructive. Young and old women surround a bizarrely gigantic he-goat representing the Devil. They are presenting him with sacrificial gifts in the form of babies and young children. The picture can also be interpreted as a coded attack on the Inquisition, the religious tribunal set up by the Catholic hierarchy to fight heresy. In Spain the Inquisition exercised a huge political and social influence. For centuries, in fact, the social and religious order had dominated the Spanish people and kept them in ignorance and superstition. The Church was therefore directly responsible for retarding the development of a freer and more enlightened Spain which Goya and his liberal friends hoped to bring about. Goya denounced the corruption of the Church in a number of works, particularly in paintings and etchings belonging to the period from *Los Caprichos* onward. However, his criticism of misused religious power was matched by his heartfelt portrayal of episodes of authentic religious heroism.

♦ **CENSORSHIP**
Publication of the etchings was announced on the front of the *Madrid Diary* newspaper. Someone reported the shop-keeper, where the etchings were on sale, to the Inquisition, which promptly removed the works from circulation as scandalous and blasphemous.

GOYA AND CHILDREN

"I have a four-year-old child who is so good-looking that everyone in the streets of Madrid stares at him," Goya wrote to his friend Zapater, with unconcealed pride. Goya had five children by Josefa, but was denied the joy of seeing his family grow up: only one of the children, Javier, actually reached adulthood and produced a grandchild. Goya portrayed children with great care and tenderness. The importance of childhood, that "fleeting golden age" as Goya called it, was beginning to be appreciated in his time, partly thanks to the great writer Jean-Jacques Rousseau, whose book *Emile* caused a great deal of controversy when it was published in 1762. Goya probably never read it, yet an affectionate concern for youthful innocence, always under threat, is tangible in all his work, from cartoons to portraits.

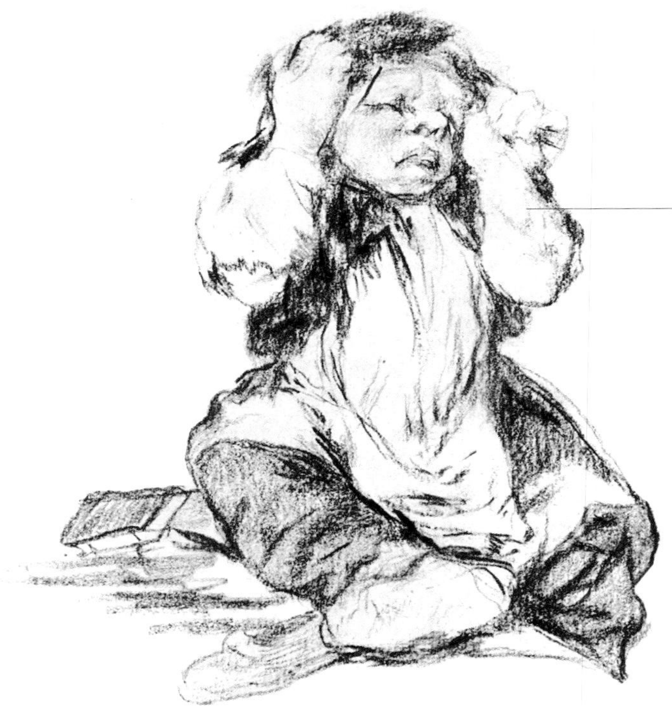

♦ **A Child's Rage** There was nothing sentimental about the way in which Goya observed and interpreted childhood. In this charcoal drawing of 1824 (Prado, Madrid), with a few simple lines, he succeeded brilliantly in conveying a child's anger.

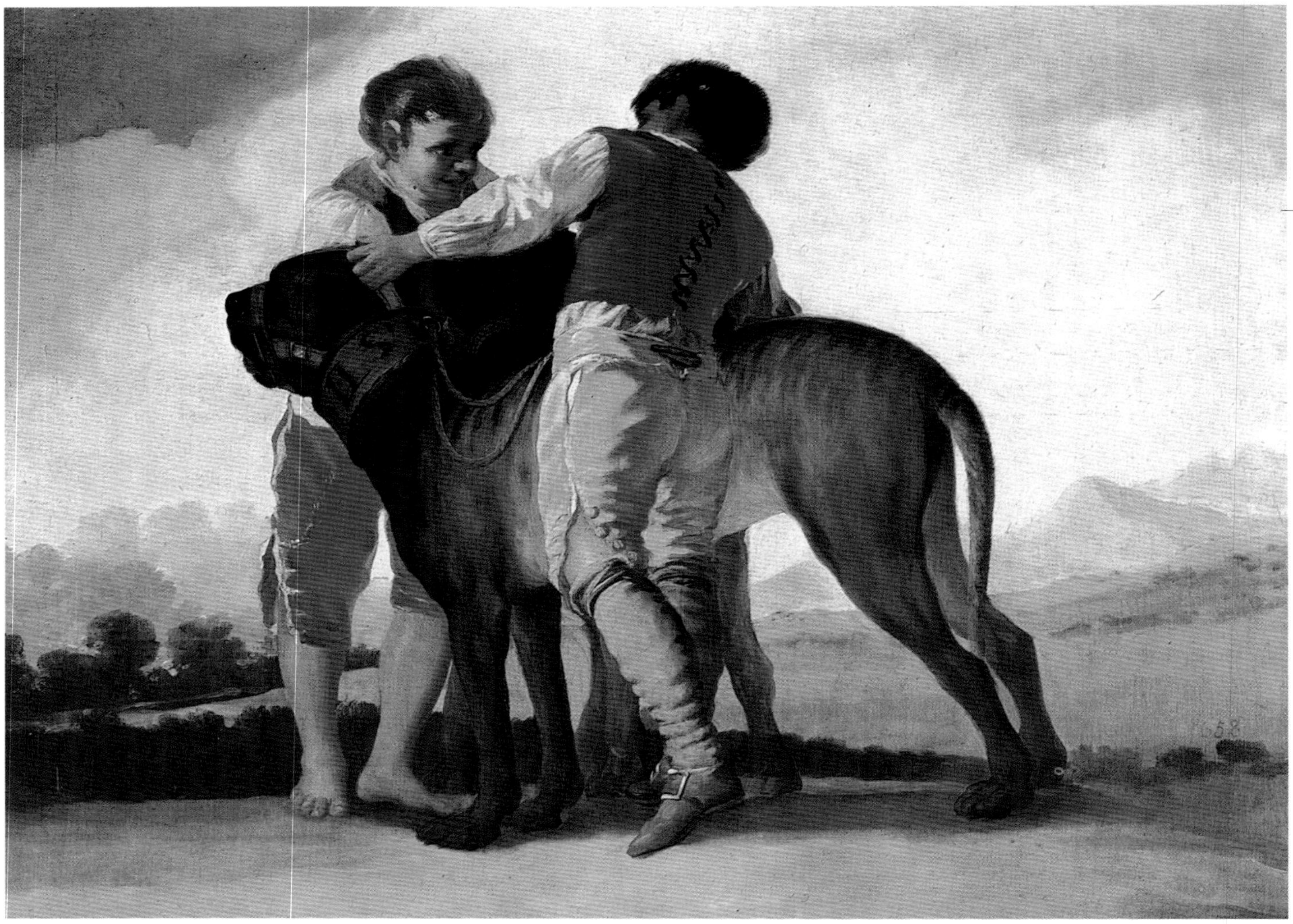

♦ **Boys with Mastiffs** 1786–87; Prado, Madrid. Among the earliest of Goya's tapestry cartoons, this playful scene expresses tension and lively movement through the use of solid volumes and skillful composition. The bright colors used for the children contrast with the browns and grays of the dogs and the ground.

11. Goya's life ♦ *1797, Madrid. The Duke and Duchess of Osuna commissioned Goya to paint witchcraft subjects, very much the vogue in the circles Goya frequented: bullfighters and actresses as well as liberal intellectuals, who were back in favor at court. Goya made superb portraits of these people. He also executed* Los Caprichos, *a series of satirical etchings published in January 1799, which caused great controversy. Copies of* Los Caprichos *were put on sale in a shop in the Calle Desengaño, where Goya had lived since 1776. The artist offered one to the king, but two weeks later* Los Caprichos *were withdrawn on the orders of the Inquisition. From this time on, Goya began to experience difficulties with the authorities.* ➳

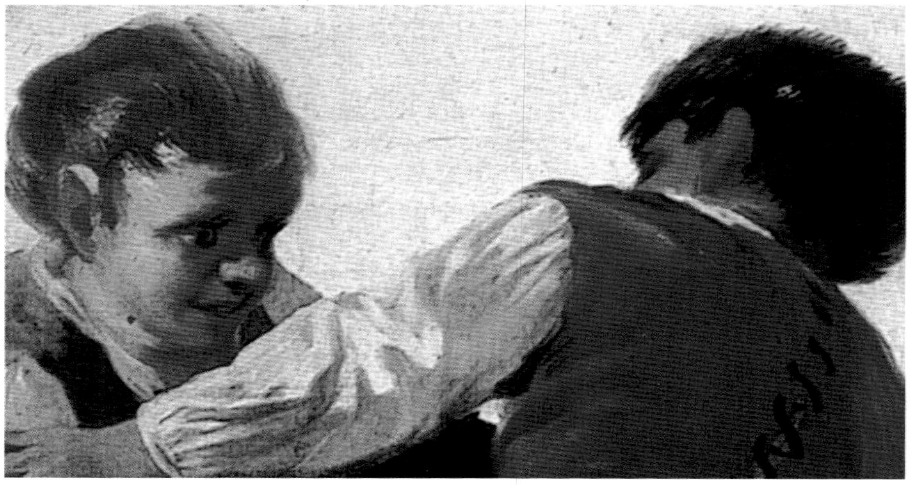

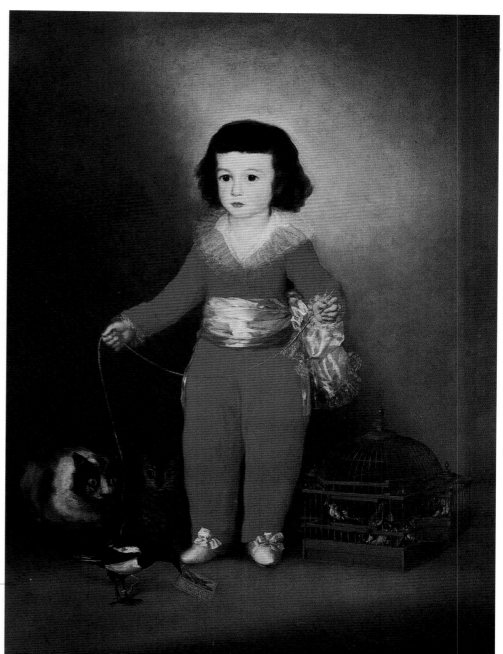

THE FRENCH REVOLUTION

In the late 18th century, France was still a rigidly divided society. An absolute monarchy ruled, with the support of the First and Second Estates – the nobility and the clergy. The Third Estate comprised the majority of the active population – peasants, artisans, merchants, and other middle-class and professional people. The Third Estate was heavily taxed but had no political rights. In May 1789, in an attempt to reverse an increasingly serious financial crisis, King Louis XVI summoned the Estates General, a consultative body which had not met for a century and a half. Here the Third Estate did have a voice, and the result was an irresistible movement in favor of social and political reform. By August 1789, the Estates General had transformed itself into a Constituent Assembly, abolished feudal privileges, and approved the Declaration of the Rights of Man. But the king's obstinacy and the sheer impetus of the Revolution led to a series of dramatic events. France became a republic, at war with most of Europe, and a period of French expansion began.

THE DEATH ♦ OF MARAT
David, 1793; Musées Royaux des Beaux Arts, Brussels. A leading figure of the French Revolution, the politician and journalist Jean Paul Marat is shown here as a revolutionary martyr. Afflicted by a skin ailment, Marat worked in his bath, where he was murdered by a noble-woman Charlotte Corday. In David's Neoclassical art, civic and political issues were given their loftiest expression.

♦ VERSAILLES
The royal family's vast residence at Versailles, southwest of Paris, symbolized the luxury that the court could afford, even when the people went hungry. Amassing troops around the palace, the king showed his intention to turn against his insolent subjects rather than accept the change to a constitutional monarchy which might have saved his throne.

12. GOYA'S LIFE ♦ *The queen's favorite, Godoy, was again in the ascendant at the Spanish court. Willingly or not, Goya became caught up in the minister's private affairs. In 1800 Godoy bought Goya's house in the Calle Desengaño, where he installed his mistress, Pepita Tudo. Here, in 1800–2, Goya portrayed Pepita naked and then, in the same pose and no less provocatively, clothed: known now all over the world, these paintings were then his most secret and "scandalous" works. During the same period Goya painted a tender and melancholy portrait of Godoy's wife, the Countess of Chinchón. Meanwhile, he himself had moved to the nearby Calle Valverde.* ➤

♦ INVADED BY WOMEN
On October 5, 1789, the women of Paris, protesting over bread shortages, marched on Versailles. After a day's walk, they clashed with troops of the Flanders regiment. Undaunted, they then invaded Versailles and forced the king and his family to return to Paris, under the eye of the revolutionaries and the National Assembly.

♦ LIBERTY LEADING THE PEOPLE
Delacroix, 1830; Louvre, Paris. Delacroix's work exalts revolutionary insurrection while also expressing patriotic sentiments. Liberty is a real woman and yet, at the same time, an idealized beauty, victoriously waving the French flag against the background of a Paris in ruins. Delacroix's artistic formation was Neoclassical, though he was the painter who best anticipated Romanticism.

LAFAYETTE ♦
The National Guard was led by the Marquis de Lafayette, who had fought for the independence of the American states.

♦ FRANCE IS SLOW TO REFORM
The 18th century was an age of great reforms – religious, political, social, economic, and legal. These reforms included the subjugation of the Church to the State; a limiting of the privileges of the nobility and clergy; an affirmation of the principle of equality; the establishment of institutions of public education; the abolition of feudal privileges and a lessening of the influence of the great landowning nobility, where serfdom still prevailed; the elimination of medieval guilds which, with their rigid regulations, inhibited the development of industry; and the codification of national laws.
In France, despite the country's wealth and large population, reform had been neglected. The king was, in theory, absolute, but in return for his political power the nobility and the Church retained huge social and economic privileges. There were many other administrative and social anomalies. Consequently, large numbers of non-noble men of wealth and education resented their lack of influence and, in the event of a crisis, might be potential leaders of the discontented workers and peasants.
When royal bankruptcy threatened and the king called the Estates General, the crisis arrived.
Above: Louis XVI.

♦ THE WOMEN OF PARIS
The Parisian women were leading figures in the Revolution. In June 1791, they were unable to prevent the king from fleeing; but this episode doomed the monarchy, eventually leading to the proclamation of the Republic and the execution of Louis XVI.

♦ THE ROYAL CARRIAGE
Louis XVI and his family were escorted to Paris by the new citizens' militia, the National Guard.

COURT LIFE

Can an artist paint a portrait that pleases the sitters yet seems to other people like a ferocious criticism or merciless caricature of its subjects and their world? That is exactly what Goya succeeded in doing in *The Family of Charles IV*, a work famous for its ambiguity. The royal family is lined up, king and princes in bemedaled uniforms, queen and princesses in dazzling gowns, posing before History. The Spanish monarchy is passing through a period of decline, but the royal family seems unaware of the fact. Behind the sumptuous fabrics, the jewels, and the decorations, we perceive empty minds and trivial personalities. With a sense of irony, Goya observes the members of a declining dynasty, laboring under the illusion that Spain is firmly under their control. In reality, their still-flickering light is about to be extinguished as the Napoleonic wind blowing across Europe approaches.

♦ MARIA LUISA AND HER DAUGHTER MARIA ISABEL
The queen's puffed, graceless face (below) contrasts with the delicate, rosy features of the girl (left). Goya has given the queen, as the dominant royal partner, an imposing if unattractive presence. The result is a clear-sighted psychological portrait. The painting is a devastating characterization of its subjects. But quite apart from its implicit moral judgments, it is fascinating for its vivid colors, the contrasts of light and shadow, and its treatment of rich fabrics, golds, and embroideries.

13. GOYA'S LIFE ♦ *Short of money, Goya accepted a proposal that he should decorate the dome of the church of San Antonio de la Florida in Madrid, an extremely difficult assignment for a man in his poor health. The result was a masterpiece of invention. In 1800, Goya was entrusted with the prestigious commission to paint a portrait of the royal family. In spite of the revolutionary upheavals in Europe, the dynasty wished to present itself as powerful and united. The painting, a work of great realism, was approved by the sovereigns, although the image created by Goya is hardly flattering.* ➽♦

♦ THE FAMILY OF CHARLES IV
1801; Prado, Madrid. Goya executed the portrait in 1801, after making a series of sketches from life. The political meaning of the work is clear: postrevolutionary Europe was being shown that the Bourbons of Spain were still unshaken. Thirteen figures of different ages are lined up in a row, their faces expressing different personalities: the candor of the children, the gaunt vacancy of the king's sister, the haughtiness of the queen, the weakness of Charles. On the left of the painting is the back of Goya's canvas. His face can just be seen in the background. In front of him stands the future King Ferdinand VII.

♦ THE MIRACLE OF ST. ANTHONY OF PADUA
1798; Cupola of San Antonio de la Florida, Manzanares. Defying convention and asserting his artistic freedom, Goya painted a group of ordinary people crowding around an imaginary balcony where St. Anthony is performing a miracle. The fresco, with its light, rapid brushwork, is an achievement of extraordinary maturity.

♦ THE TYRANT
1799; Academy of San Fernando. The actress María del Rosario Fernandez was nicknamed "the tyrant" because her husband, also a well-known actor, usually played the part of a tyrannical ruler. The rendering of light and color is splendid, especially in the lower part of the dress.

GENERAL ♦ ANTONIO RICARDOS
1793–94; Prado, Madrid. Having won an important battle in 1793, during the Franco-Spanish war, General Ricardos became a national hero. Goya portrays him as full of dignity and pride. His forehead is lighter than his face because he usually wore a hat. The clothes and chair are superbly rendered.

THE DUCHESS OF ALBA

Beautiful, eccentric, and provocative, María Teresa Cayetana de Silva, the thirteenth Duchess of Alba, was in the public eye more than any other woman in Spain except the queen. She was a flamboyant character who shared the easy ways and colorful language of the dandified girls and young men of the city, the *majas* and *majos*. Her charm and her contempt for convention seduced ministers, bull-fighters, and students alike. And probably Goya, too. They met in 1795, when he was commissioned to paint her portrait. They spent a summer in her palace in Sanlucàr, after she had become a widow. He painted and drew her, sometimes in private, informal poses. But the paintings and drawings are the only basis for the belief that Goya had a passion for the duchess, or that, for a time at least, his feelings were returned. The portrait of her in black bears the inscription "only Goya," written in the artist's hand, together with their names, next to each other, on her rings.

♦ **THE DUCHESS OF ALBA**
The portrait on the right (private collection, Madrid), dated 1795, is a celebration in light, luminous colors. Stately in white, which highlights her femininity, the duchess dominates the canvas with an imperious gesture of the hand. The portrait on the left, dated 1797, hangs today in the Hispanic Society, New York. The duchess is enveloped in a black lace mantilla, which matches her dress. She has a more apprehensive air, although she is as imposing as ever. In the two rings on her fingers, the artist has written "Alba" and "Goya."

14. GOYA'S LIFE ♦ *The military expansion of revolutionary and later Napoleonic France influenced Spanish history deeply. In 1808, the French emperor, Napoleon, secured the abdication of Charles IV and his son Ferdinand, replacing them with his own brother, Joseph Bonaparte. Popular uprisings against the French were supported by British forces, leading to terrible bloodshed, atrocities, and reprisals. Though Goya believed in a constitutional monarchy rather than the absolute rule of the Bourbon kings, he sympathized with the uprising, but, as his* Disasters of War *make clear, he was horrified by the inhuman behavior of both sides. His work during the war often represented a deeply personal response to events.* ➡

♦ **PROUD BEAUTY**
The 1795 portrait shows the duchess with a luminous complexion, large, dark eyes, and a mass of black hair. Her necklace and the ribbon in her hair are the same bright red as the bow on her bodice. She has the air of a Mediterranean beauty, proud but not haughty, immediately alluring.

◆ **SELF-PORTRAIT**
1795; Metropolitan Museum, New York.
At the time of his relationship with the Duchess of Alba, Goya was over fifty years old.

He was seriously affected by deafness, and his face was marked by suffering. Yet he possessed a power of attraction that he would not lose even in old age.

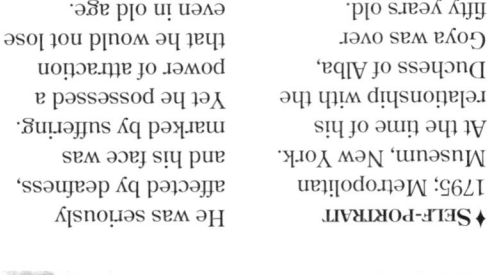

◆ **THE DUCHESS WITH HER CHAPERONE**
1795; Prado, Madrid.
There is a satirical tone to this oddly informal and intimate scene. The duchess, seen from behind, her black head against the almost equally black background, makes a gesture that sends the old woman reeling backward. With a stick in one hand, and a crucifix in the other, the woman looks as though she is trying to drive back a devil.

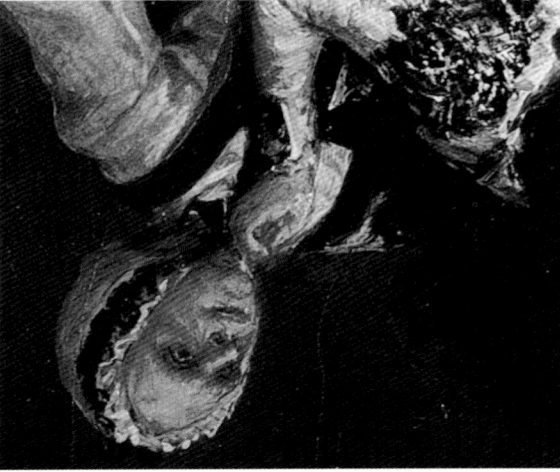

◆ **THE CHAPERONE**
This detail shows the face of the chaperone: the eyes staring and alarmed, the head enclosed in a bonnet. With just a few brushstrokes the expression is fixed and the character defined. Because of her piety, the woman was nicknamed "the blessed one."

◆ **THE DUCHESS OF ALBA ARRANGES HER HAIR**
1796–97; Biblioteca Nacional, Madrid.
The thick, black, wavy hair of the duchess is the main feature of this fine, very freely executed ink drawing.

◆ **THE DUCHESS'S SOCIAL CIRCLE**
Goya was friendly with the Duchess of Alba's circle, most of whom were not of noble birth. The duchess was deeply attracted to the world of the matadors, or bullfighter's, idols of the crowd. She was a woman who placed a high value on Spanish tradition. She dressed like a *maja*, went to the bullfights, and exulted in the feats of the famous Romero brothers – particularly the magnificent Pedro (above). The Romero brothers were innovators who created a new style of bullfighting and were admired by the crowd for their courage and technical mastery. Pedro Romero was patronized by the Duchess of Alba, while the Duchess of Osuna supported Mariano Ceballos, a native American Indian. The two noblewomen were rivals who strove against each other even through their favorites. Goya too was a bullfighting enthusiast, as his sketches and drawings make very clear.

Above: A portrait by Goya of the matador Pedro Romero, 1795–98; Kimbell Art Museum, Fortworth.

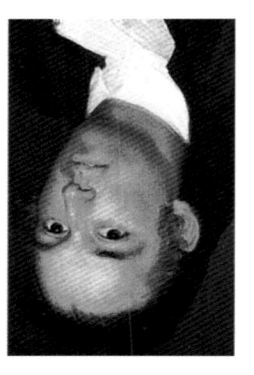

CONTEMPORARY EUROPEAN ART

The Neoclassical art popularized by Winckelmann and Mengs and practiced by the leading artists of the second half of the 18th century took Greek and Roman works as its sources of inspiration. Neoclassicism also served as a medium for historical and social ideas, many of them generated by the French Revolution. Artists such as David and Canova portrayed the great figures of the age on canvas and in marble, turning them into heroes and moral examples that were intended to stand alongside those of antiquity. But there were other works in which sentiment and emotion prevailed. There was no absolute distinction between the two. Neoclassical art merged into Romantic art, which exalted the individual soul and nature, and was increasingly open to formal and thematic innovations. The serenity to which classical art aspired was disturbed by the violence of history itself, and by the reemergence in the European mind of fantastic, irrational visions. Both outlooks existed side by side in the work of Goya himself.

♦ HEROIC CONQUEROR
Jacques-Louis David, *Napoleon Crossing the Alps*, 1801; Musée National du Château de Malmaison, Rueil. After studying in Rome, David (1748–1825) became famous as a Neoclassical painter of episodes from ancient history. He took part in the French Revolution and was later made "First Painter" by Napoleon, whose career of conquest is compared with those of the heroes of antiquity in paintings such as this. David's example spread the idea of art as a form of moral teaching and historical record.

ROMANTIC ♦
LANDSCAPES
1. John Constable, *Trees at Hampstead* (detail), 1821; Victoria and Albert Museum, London.
2. Caspar David Friedrich, *Abbey in the Oak Wood*, 1809–10; Staatliche Museen, Berlin.
3 Joseph Mallord William Turner, *Buttermere Lake*, 1798; Tate Gallery, London.

HUMAN HISTORY ♦
1. Hubert Robert, *Design for the Decoration of the Great Gallery of the Louvre in 1796* (detail); Louvre, Paris.
2. Jacques-Louis David, *The Sabine Women*, 1799; Louvre, Paris.
3. Théodore Géricault, *The Raft of the "Medusa,"* 1819; Louvre, Paris.

NEOCLASSICAL NUDES ♦
1. Antonio Canova, *Pauline Borghese as Venus* (detail), 1804–8; Galleria Borghese, Rome.
2. Antonio Canova, *Cupid Waking Psyche with a Kiss*, 1787–93; Louvre, Paris.
3. Jean-Auguste-Dominique Ingres, *Bather of Valpinçon*, 1808; Louvre, Paris.

THE MAJAS

A naked young woman, lying on soft cushions, poses for the artist. She looks straight at him, conscious of the beauty and sensuality of her own smooth, glowing body. Goya portrayed her figure realistically, and this caused something of a scandal. Nudes were rare in Spanish painting, since they were strongly suspected of being immoral. Goya's greatest predecessor, Velázquez, had painted a naked Venus, but his figure could be passed off as a mythical one, made respectable by its association with classical antiquity. Goya, a century and a half later, had no time for hypocrisy, for realism was central to his art. His *maja* was therefore a real, living woman. When, the following year, he portrayed her in the same pose but dressed, he again made her an extremely sensual figure, charged with an unmistakable erotic appeal.

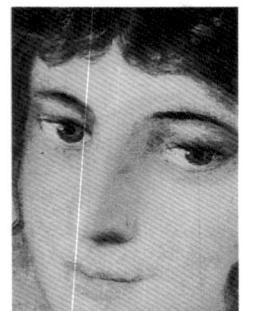

♦ **THE NAKED MAJA**
1800; Prado, Madrid. Goya painted this, his most famous picture, for the queen's favorite, Godoy, who also bought Goya's house, number 2 in the Calle Desengaño, for Pepita Tudo, the model who posed for *The Naked Maja*. Godoy was very pleased with the painting and asked Goya to make a copy of it but with the model dressed. The two works were probably placed one above the other in the study of the minister, who could leave the less explicit one on display and only reveal the nude in private, by operating a spring mechanism. Goya was denounced to the Inquisition for having produced "obscene pictures," but the protection of his patron, who possessed a secret collection of nudes, shielded him from any serious difficulties with the law. After Godoy's death, the work was put away in a cupboard at the Academy and shown to the public only in 1900, when it was exhibited with its companion piece, *The Clothed Maja*. A century after Goya painted it, the Spanish people were finally able to see a work which was immediately acclaimed as one of the finest items in their entire artistic heritage. A year later, in 1901, the two paintings were hung in the Prado, where they are still a major attraction for visitors.

♦ **ANALOGIES**
This is another example of Fuseli and Goya, artists geographically distant from each other, though close in terms of taste and inspiration, choosing similar subjects for their works. This is Fuseli's *Reclining Nude and Piano Player,* 1799–1800; Offentliche Kunstsammlung, Basel.

The Clothed Maja *was painted in a free, brilliant, light-catching style, which reveals the painter's intense interest in the texture and sheen of the* maja's *garments. These are so superbly rendered that it seems almost possible to touch them. By contrast,* The Naked Maja *is much more refined, and also more well-defined: here Goya masterfully reproduces the transparency of the* maja's *skin, the freshness of her flesh, and the splendor of her complexion, which is* highlighted by the rich blue of the velvet couch and the dark background. One critic remarked that the *maja* seemed as though made of porcelain, while another wrote that she seemed "to be modeled in wax." The composition of the painting is based on a diagonal arrangement: the figure is positioned so that the left knee comes slightly forward toward the observer, while the eyes, although looking in the same general direction, give a more sidelong glance, which preserves a sense of mystery.

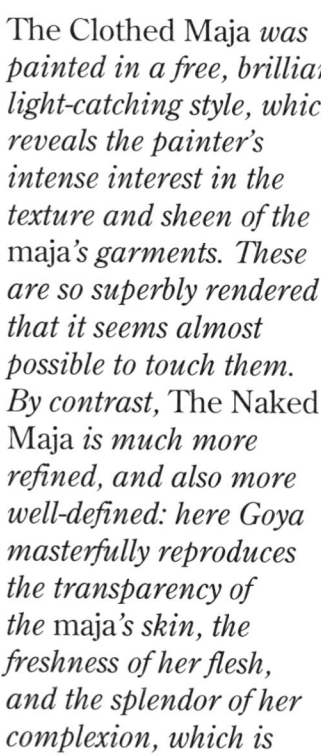

♦ **CHARM**
The delicate face with rounded cheekbones, the thin, straight nose, the almond eyes, the small, well-drawn mouth: this is certainly no ordinary beauty. The *maja*'s expression has been interpreted in various ways: is it inviting or detached? Whichever may be the case, it is fascinating.

Velázquez, *The Toilet of Venus at the Mirror,* 1645–48; National Gallery, London. Venus, with her narrow waist and rounded hips, is turned away from the spectator, but her face is visible, pensive, and slightly out of focus, in the reflection of the mirror held firmly by a cupid. Note the splendid harmony of the colors in this work, which is also known as "The Rokeby Venus."

♦ **CLOTHED AND NAKED**

The Clothed Maja (far left) was a copy of *The Naked Maja* (left). The model, Pepita Tudo, lies in a languid pose, as if offering herself. She is not at all idealized, but represented with frank realism. Yet Goya's paintbrush seems to caress the beautiful body, which can be imagined beneath the garments represented in detail in *The Clothed Maja*: the gaudy little jacket, the sash, and the filmy, white, figure-hugging clothes.

♦ **OLYMPIA**

Manet, 1863; Musée d'Orsay, Paris. Although representations of the nude were accepted in France, this picture was greeted with outrage when it was exhibited at the Paris Salon in 1865. The face is wide and sensual and the body is represented without recourse to chiaroscuro. The nude is shame-free.

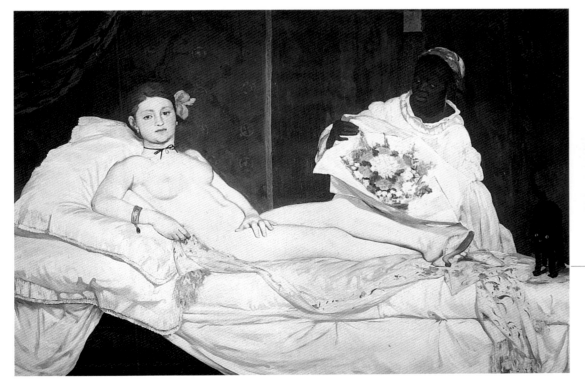

THE PORTRAITS

The greatest portrait painters have aimed not only to capture the physical likeness of their sitters, but also to interpret their characters and personalities. The clothes and the pose assumed by the person portrayed often tell us something about his or her social status, sense of self-worth, and profession. Goya was a master at conveying such things. Of the huge number of portraits he executed, almost all were of a very high standard with regard to the psychological makeup of his subjects, especially when they were people with whom he was on close terms. In his portrait of the Marquesa de la Solana, who had only a few months to live, Goya captured the lady's pride in the face of her illness, by means of restrained colors and an upright, stoic stance. By contrast, in painting the young Count Nuñez, he captured the elegance that was the man's dominant feature. In his portraits of fair ladies, he brought out their vivacity or apprehension, giving them expressions that were either melancholy or full of the joy of living, in either case providing us with windows into their souls.

♦ **MARIA ANA DE PONTEJOS Y SANDOVAL**
1786; National Gallery, Washington, D.C. This portrait of the sister-in-law of the Count of Floridablanca is a curiosity because of the contrast between the cold formality of the woman's expression and the vivid, meticulous treatment of the rest, blending lovely grays, pinks, and greens.

♦ **ISABEL DE PORCEL**
1804–5; National Gallery, London. This is one of Goya's finest portraits. The splendid lady has followed aristocratic fashion by adopting the traditional dress of the *majas*: a tight-fitting bodice and a black shawl (mantilla) worn over the head. The Duchess of Alba and even the queen also had themselves portrayed in this way. Note the magnificent contrast of black and pink. Isabel's face has well-marked features, and her very fair skin shines out from the ivory blackness of the mantilla.

♦ **YOUNG WOMAN WITH A FAN**
1805–6; National Gallery, Washington, D.C. This typically Spanish beauty may have been the wife of the bookseller Antonio Bailó, who testified on Goya's behalf during the proceedings brought against him by the Inquisition after he had caused a scandal by publishing *Los Caprichos*.

♦ **YOUNG MEN**
Left: Don Pantaleón
Pérez de Nenín,
1808; Banco
Exterior, Madrid.
The burly major-
general of hussars
was in charge of
forces raised in
Bilbao, and probably
came from that city.

Below: Count
Fernan Nuñez, 1803;
private collection,
Madrid. The count
wears the cape of a
hidalgo and his
well-shaped leg is
sheathed in white
pants. His young
face is framed by
a tricornered hat.
Again, Goya chooses
dark colors, and
favors black – the
most Goyesque color
and the one most
characteristic of the
artist's mature years.

♦ **DONA RITA
BARRENECHEA**
*The Marquesa
de la Solana*, 1794–95;
Louvre, Paris.
A friend of the
Duchess of Alba,
the Marquesa died
at the age of 28,
shortly after Goya
painted this portrait.
Over her black dress
she wears a pale
mantilla, which eases
the transition to the
subtly modulated
color tones of blue
and gray. The only
bright note is the
spectacular pink
ribbon.

♦ **FRANCISCA SABASA
Y GARCIA**
1808; National Gallery,
Washington, D.C.
This is a classical
pose, with the hands
clasped and the face
framed by a scarf. The
colors are sober and
soft, giving emphasis
to the pale gloves and
the pretty face, with its
innocent, serious, and
pensive expression.
Nothing distracts us
from the girl herself,
emerging from the
dark background.
The rendering of
her features, the
balance of the
composition, and
the characterization
are beyond reproach.

GUERRILLA WARFARE AGAINST THE INVADER

♦ THE EUROPEAN
SITUATION
In revolutionary
France the coup d'état
launched by General
Napoleon Bonaparte
in November 1799
ended political
conflict in the country
and marked the
beginning of years of
expansion. Napoleon,
First Consul and then
Emperor of France,
won a series of great
military victories and
soon redrew the
political map of
Europe. Through
annexations and
the granting of
constitutions to
satellite kingdoms,
the achievements of
the French Revolution
were spread across
western Europe:
abolition of slavery
and feudalism,
affirmation of
property rights, and
equality before
the law.
However, the British
opposed Napoleon
and a war of blockade
and counter-blockade
ensued. Spain became
a victim of the clash
between the two great
powers. Although his
Bourbon relatives
perished in the French
Revolution, Charles IV
was forced into an
alliance with France.
Yet this failed to save
the monarchy when
Napoleon decided to
place his brother,
Joseph, on the throne.
Liberals such as Goya
admired French
institutions and had
hoped to introduce
them in Spain; but the
arrival of the French
as invaders shocked
and disillusioned
them.
Above: detail of
*Manuel Godoy on the
Field of Battle*, 1801;
Academy of San
Fernando, Madrid.

In November 1807, the French army crossed the
territory of their Spanish allies and occupied Lisbon,
to seal off England's trading outlets. A few months
later, the French emperor, Napoleon, intervened in
the internal conflict between Charles IV and his son
Ferdinand, thrusting both aside and conferring the
Spanish crown on his own brother, Joseph. But even
before Joseph reached Madrid in May 1808, the entire
country had risen up against the French troops.
The British expeditionary force which had fought
in Portugal supported the rebels. Napoleon himself
hurried to put his brother back on the throne
and, in February 1809, the revolt seemed to have
been quelled. But throughout the peninsula a
fierce guerrilla resistance developed, to which
the occupiers responded with merciless
repression. Goya bore witness to the next
three years of violence and tyranny with
an outpouring of extraordinary images.

♦ SPANISH REBELS
MAKING BULLETS
1812–13; Palacio
Real, Madrid.

♦ THE FRENCH ARMY
Irresistible in the open
field, the army was
vulnerable to
unexpected strikes
on the rough
terrain of the
Aragonese
countryside.

RUDIMENTARY ♦
WEAPONS
Simple weapons
and bullets were
handmade, but
extremely effective.

♦ **SPANISH REBELS
MAKING GUNPOWDER**
1812–13; Palacio
Real, Madrid.

♦ **RESISTANCE**
In the Spanish
countryside, a group
of peasants organizes
an ambush against
the Napoleonic army,
which is encamped
in the near distance.

♦ **AN EVERYDAY WAR**
The people in arms
concealed the
preparation of
guerrilla warfare
behind the apparent
normality of their
daily activities.

15. GOYA'S LIFE ♦ *In 1812 Goya mourned the death
of his wife Josefa, with whom he had lived for almost
forty years. After this event, he made an inventory of
his possessions, sharing half of his estate, which
amounted to about 360,000 reals, with his son Javier.
In the meantime Javier had married Gumersinda
Goicoechea, who belonged to a wealthy merchant family.
The child of this marriage was Mariano, a beautiful boy
whom Goya loved dearly. Nevertheless, during this
period, Goya was inevitably preoccupied with the tragedy
being enacted in Spain, and, although his own
circumstances remained comfortable, the horrors of
the war were reflected in his work.* ➢♦

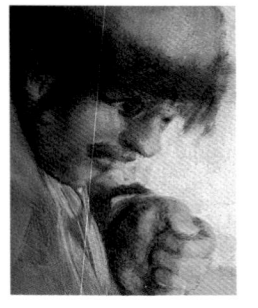

THE THIRD OF MAY 1808

May 2 and 3, 1808, were among the most dramatic days of the entire war in Spain. Charles IV and Ferdinand had already been summoned to Bayonne by Napoleon; when the other Spanish princes were ordered to leave for the frontier, riots erupted in Madrid. By May 2, these had turned into a full-scale insurrection against the French forces in the city, which only regained control after a good deal of bloodshed. On May 3, firing squads began to execute the rebels in batches. It was enough to be found in possession of a weapon to be shot on the spot. Much later, Goya created his own dramatic version of these events. His painting, *The Third of May 1808,* became a symbol of humanity oppressed by violence: it was a cry of despair and a manifesto that would echo into the 20th century.

♦ **THE WORK**
The Third of May 1808, 1814; oil on canvas, 8 ft 8 in x 11 ft 4 in (266 x 345 cm); Prado, Madrid. From 1808, Goya was distressed by the terrible times his country was living through, although, as a professional artist, he worked for whichever regime was in power. Spain continued to be torn apart by atrocities, reprisals, instability, the marching and countermarching of foreign armies who fed off the people, looting, torture, and murder. In 1814, during the inter-regnum between the expulsion of the French and the return of the Bourbon, Ferdinand VII, a ruling council was set up, presided over by the Cardinal of Bourbon. Goya petitioned for funds that would enable him to commemorate "the most valorous and heroic actions of our glorious insurrection against the tyrant of Europe," Napoleon. His proposal was accepted, and he executed this work and *The Second of May 1808*, which pictured a street battle between a squadron of Mameluke (Egyptian) cavalry and the Madrid mob. The paintings were displayed during the commemorative celebrations on May 2 and 3. The two canvases can be seen at the Prado Museum, where *The Third of May 1808* is one of the most popular and admired works on display.

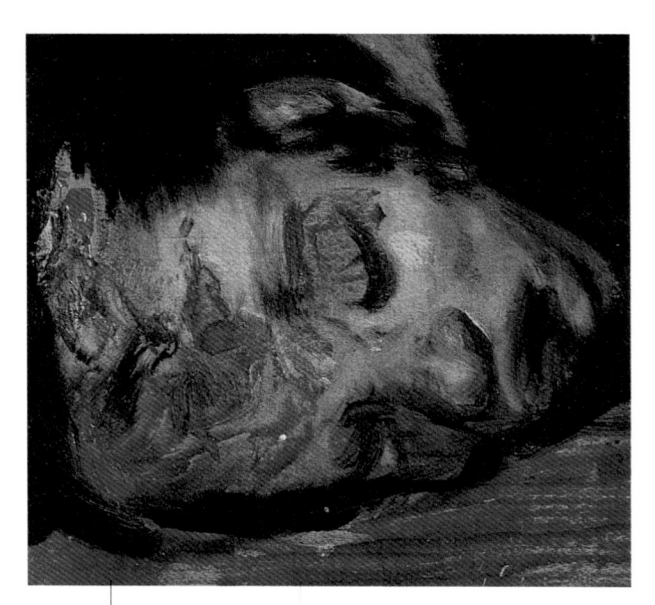

♦ **ONE OF THE DEAD**
A man has already fallen under the fire of the French soldiers. Sunk in the blood and mud, his arms flung out in front of him, he has been deprived of his identity and is now just one among the corpses heaped up on the execution ground.

Against the background of a ghostlike city, the massacre is carried out by the yellow light of a large lamp. All around the terrifed victims is the darkness of night, which can also be regarded as symbolizing "the sleep of reason." The spectator's eye is irresistibly drawn to the white shirt of the man with his arms raised, who is about to be martyred.

The painting is full of superb artistic effects, but Goya does not allow the chiaroscuro and other aspects of his virtuosity to absorb our attention. Instead, he presents a scene notable for its harsh realism — an event that we would rather not witness, but one that was part of the "nightmare of history" and therefore must be put on record and condemned.

A fraction of a second and the bullets will hit the man on the left, who is standing with outstretched arms. His petrified face and gesture of desperation bring home the horror of the event. It is not presented in a romantic or heroic light, and any sense of glory or patriotic ardor has been eliminated. Goya's realism and disenchantment offer a harsh lesson to humanity. The faceless soldiers are puppets in uniform, worked by unseen, impersonal forces.

THE EXECUTION OF ♦ MAXIMILIAN OF MEXICO
1867; Kunsthalle, Mannheim. In this painting the French artist Manet (1832–83) was certainly inspired by Goya, whom he regarded as one of his masters. The composition is similar to *The Third of May,* while the curious onlookers above the wall are reminiscent of those in Goya's bullfighting scenes. In the detail, the soldier loads his rifle, as if detached from the execution that is being carried out.

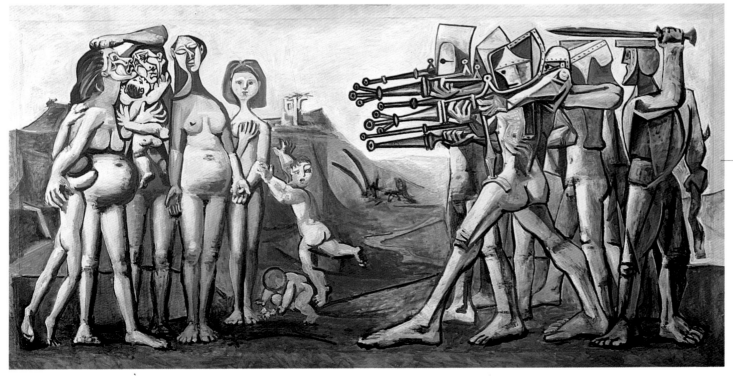

♦ MASSACRE IN KOREA
1951; Musée Picasso, Paris. Once again, in this work by Picasso, menacing, robotlike soldiers point their weapons at a line of victims. This time the victims are women, children, and babies, represented as naked and therefore at their most harmless and vulnerable. Although inspired by the Korean War (1950–53), this is a work beyond time; it condemns every war and sides with humanity against violence. The grouping is like that of *The Third of May.* Picasso, a Spaniard, felt very close to Goya.

THE DISASTERS OF WAR

♦ GOYA'S TECHNIQUE
FOR THE ETCHINGS
Goya displayed an
extraordinary ability
to take the measure
of his own times,
to bear witness to
the great events of
history, and to put
on record the
habits and customs
of the people.
To reveal the
turmoil of his
feelings and
the urgency of his
ideas, he adopted
a technique that
served his purpose
perfectly.
The technique was
etching combined
with aquatint. It
involved "drawing"
with a needle on a
copper plate, then
inking the plate and
pressing it onto
paper to make
the print.
Goya had used the
technique to great
effect in *Los Caprichos,*
and returned to it for
The Disasters.
Here his mastery
of the medium
reached even greater
heights, with an
even more intense
line, a more
dramatic chiaroscuro,
and images of
terrible emotional
power.
These works were
evidently felt to be
subversive, since
the copper plates
of *The Disasters of
War* were kept under
lock and key
until 1854.
Not until twenty-six
years after the
artist's death
were they revealed
to the Spanish
people and to
the world.

Above: *Sad
Presentiments of What
is About to Happen;*
Prado, Madrid.

Truth is dead, according to the caption of one etching
by Goya. Anguish and despair are expressed in many of
his works from this, the most tormented period of his
life and a terrible phase in the history of Spain. His
response to the traumatic events of the time appears
above all in a series of etchings called *The Disasters of
War,* produced over about ten years. Goya must have
seen many of the scenes in these etchings with his own
eyes: the siege of Saragossa, the masses in revolt,
people hunger-stricken, raped, and killed – and not only
by the enemy, for, in war, violence is not confined to one
side. The series also includes works of social criticism
and attacks on the reactionary influence of the Church,
which became as strong as ever after the Bourbons had
been restored. Ever more detached from the life of the
court, Goya felt free to express himself, to take a stand
against barbarism: once again, etching was the
technique most suited to these "private" works, which
were certainly not designed to appeal to the authorities.

♦ FOR A KNIFE
Possession of any
kind of weapon,
even an ordinary
knife, was enough
to bring one to
the scaffold.
Strangulation by
means of the garrotte
was a terrifying
punishment that
ensured a slow death.

♦ MARTYRS
Naked corpses
hanging from trees
and severed heads
and limbs are dire
warnings to
passers-by.

Before Goya,
painters had depicted
horrors of this kind
only in relation to
Christian martyrs
or visions of the
Last Judgment.

♦ FOUR HORRORS
Clockwise, from
top left: *What Worse
Thing Could Be
Done?; This is
Worse; Why?;* and –

one of the most
horrific works in
the *Disasters of War*
series – Plate 39:
*A Heroic Feat! With
Dead Men!*

♦ **MAJAS ON A BALCONY**
1808–12; Metropolitan Museum, New York. During the period when he was working on *The Disasters,* Goya did some paintings of Spanish life and customs. In this one a mysterious atmosphere is created by the inviting faces of the two women and by the silhouettes of the men behind them.

♦ **THE CARNIVOROUS VULTURE**
The monster is confronted by a man of the people, while others flee in terror. Does the vulture represent imperial power, bad government, or religious oppression? Whatever it symbolizes, it is a danger, a horrendous enemy.

WHAT COURAGE! ♦
This preparatory drawing for one of the etchings in *The Disasters* shows an episode from the siege of Saragossa. Since all the soldiers manning an artillery piece have been killed, Augustina de Aragon fires the cannon and becomes a national heroine.

♦ **MAY THE ROPE BREAK!**
An imaginary street scene: a dignitary of the Church balances precariously on a tightrope in attempting to save himself from the hostile crowd below. The etching is a clear expression of Goya's hostility toward the Church, which recovered much of its former power when the Bourbons regained the throne. Even the Inquisition was revived and again suppressed freedom of thought.

16. GOYA'S LIFE ♦ *In 1812, after the French had finally been expelled by British forces commanded by the Duke of Wellington, Spain was given a liberal constitution. Goya certainly approved, and painted an* Allegory of the Constitution. *But then the Bourbons returned in the person of Ferdinand VII, the constitution was suppressed, and Spain was again subjected to an absolute monarchy and the Inquisition. Goya had to work for the new king, and painted several portraits of the victorious Duke of Wellington, whom he is said to have detested.* ➡

THE GIANT

Nightmare, vision, or metaphor? What meaning can be attributed to the image that dominates one of Goya's most fascinating and enigmatic paintings? There is no certain answer to the mystery. The procession crossing the plain is confronted by an enormous figure that towers above the horizon and invades the sky. Its back is turned, but we can see the profile of the bearded face, the raised arm, the menacing fist. Panic causes animals and carts to flee in confusion, and even the clouds seem to speed away. Is the Giant the god of war, or an image of War itself? Is it a symbol of fear, or does it represent the genius of Spain, or the strength of its people? There are many different interpretations. It is possible to argue that, on closer observation, the Giant is not such a frightening figure. Painted during the French occupation, the picture certainly seems to embody the great drama that Spain was living through.

♦ **THE GIANT**
1808–12; oil on canvas, 3 ft 9 in x 3 ft 5 in (116 x 105 cm); Prado, Madrid.
The Giant is one of the hardest of all Goya's works to decipher. There are no documents or records that can provide reliable information about the artist's inspiration, let alone tell us the precise meaning of the picture. The same can be said about some other works, such as *The City on a Rock*, which dates from the same period (and is not attributed with absolute certainty to Goya). Goya was strongly drawn to imaginary, often fantastic scenes, set in wide open spaces. For him, the sky seems to have been a stage setting full of infinite possibilities, a place of dreams, nightmares, obsessions, and supernatural apparitions: flying creatures, birds, witches, and beasts. The sky is also the element in which Goya's creatures exhibit an irresistible desire to fly, which is referred to several times in his work. A celebrated example is the *Ascension in a Montgolfier Balloon*, executed in 1813–15 (above). The hot-air balloon was a recent invention, dating from the late 18th century. It seems that the French used one of these means of aerial locomotion to chart the movement of Murat's troops in Spain from the air. It is possible that Goya had seen it and been suitably impressed.

As a work of art, The Giant *is a painting of a very high quality. The composition is dominated by the central figure, looming above the horizon and filling the sky; the rout of fleeing people and animals balances it by creating a strong sense of movement. The paint has been laid on with vigorous strokes of the brush. A superbly rendered veil of gray, white, and pinkish clouds seems to have been driven by the wind across the Giant's powerful body.*

♦ **AN ENIGMATIC EXPRESSION**
The Giant, also known as "The Colossus," is an ambiguous figure. His lowered eyelids and general expression are not particularly suggestive of ferocity or wickedness. Even his fighting stance can be seen as that of a creature prepared to defend himself, rather than one about to do evil.

♦ **FLIGHT**
The effects of the Giant's presence can be clearly seen: the huge and unexpected apparition is spreading terror. Goya creates a sense of blind movement, depicting the dramatic flight of people, vehicles, and animals. Only a mule remains motionless in the midst of the general stampede, perhaps a sign of obstinacy or stupidity. Goya was obsessed by the subject of the Giant, which he took up several times.

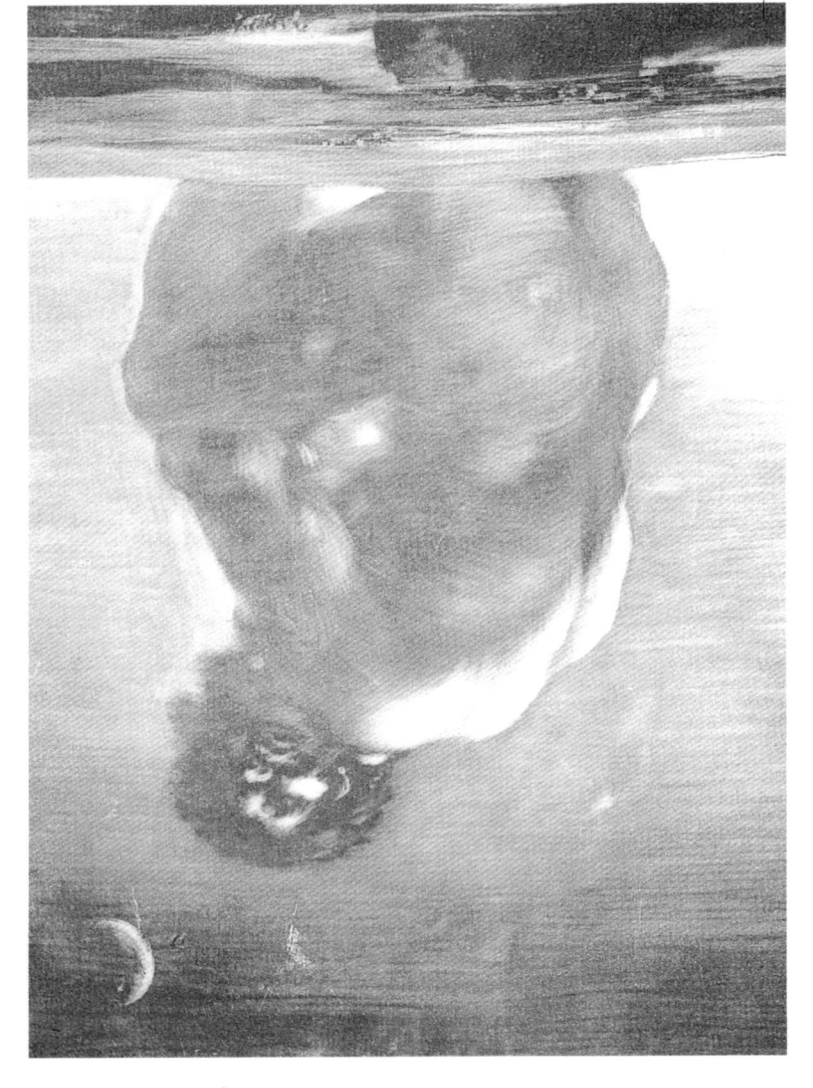

♦ THE GIANT
1810–18; Bibliothèque Nationale, Paris.
The technique used here is a form of engraving known as mezzotint. More peaceful than his painted counterpart, this giant is sitting on the edge of the Earth, beneath a crescent moon, and thinking unknowable thoughts.

♦ THE CITY ON A ROCK
1813-16; Metropolitan Museum, New York.
Another powerfully fantastic vision. The grandeur, atmosphere of suspense, and sense of silence and mystery make this work comparable with *The Giant.*

♦ THE BURIAL OF THE SARDINE
1812-14; Academy of San Fernando, Madrid. The burial of the sardine was a comic ritual that took place at the end of the Ash Wednesday carnival in Madrid. One interpretation of the painting is that it celebrated the liberation of Spain from the French. On the other hand, there is a sinister air about the masks and merry-making, suggesting a certain ambiguity in Goya's attitude.

THE "BLACK PAINTINGS"

♦ **TECHNIQUES**
Most of the "black paintings" were executed in oil and tempera. For the black areas, which are dominant throughout the series, Goya used a thick ink of the kind used by printers, which, over time, becomes even darker.

A thorough examination of the works has revealed that Goya initially painted landscapes and other relatively tranquil scenes on the walls. We do not know whether any specific event induced him to replace them with the nightmare vision of the black paintings. He may have been influenced by political events, or by his own problems with the authorities. Goya was still Court Painter, but his sympathy with the liberals, who were persecuted after the Restoration as enemies of the regime, made life difficult and eventually this caused him to leave Spain. In 1873, the paintings were in such a bad condition that it was decided to remove them from the Quinta del Sordo, in order to save them. To achieve this, it was necessary to demolish the building and conduct a delicate transfer of the paintings from the wall plaster on to canvas. The paintings were then given to the Prado Museum in Madrid. Above: a detail from *Asmodea*.

In 1819, Goya moved into a house on the banks of the Manzanares River. A deaf man had lived in it, and so it was already known as the "Quinta del Sordo" (the House of the Deaf Man). Whether the highly appropriate name influenced Goya, himself deaf since 1793, is not known. Once the purchase was completed, he improved and decorated the house. Then, ignoring the outside world, he began to work like a madman. Consequently, what he painted there lived with him and enveloped him, making constant contact with his eyes and spirit. Goya painted seven compositions on each of the two floors, filling the spaces between the doors and windows: a total surface area of 366 square feet (34 square meters). The pictures, known as the "black paintings," are terrible, delirious scenes of witchcraft, exorcism, and nightmares. The colors are very dark: blacks as dense as tar, upon which cold whites, blood reds, ochers, and yellows break out like flashes of light, revealing a dark landscape of evil and despair.

♦ **DOG**
Shown in profile, this dog is an enigmatic creature. We will never know whether it has been abandoned, or is waiting with desperate patience for some hoped-for person or event. Whichever it may be, it is a memorable image of anguish and solitude.

♦ **ASMODEA**
In this painting, two figures float in the air, with a strangely shaped rock in the background. Although a fantasy, it may also allude to the Rock of Gibraltar, where many liberals took refuge after 1815. The detail (above) shows a group of men and carts on the road, perhaps in flight. The work is disturbing, but has a compelling beauty and luminosity.

♦ TWO OLD MEN
Another grotesque and chilling image. One of the figures, obscene and insinuating, whispers something in the ear of his companion, who is leaning on a long stick. Such images leave little doubt that the black paintings were the work of an artist who was utterly obsessed by evil.

LEOCADIA ♦
Goya's young companion, dressed and veiled in black, is leaning against a tomb. Recent research has shown that Leocadia was originally painted unveiled and not in black (and therefore not in mourning), in front of a fireplace. Perhaps it was Goya himself, in a fit of depression, who transformed her; but it is equally possible that the modification was made by someone else after Goya's death.

♦ SATURN
One of the most ghoulish figures of the cycle of black paintings.
Saturn was the god of classical antiquity who, according to legend, devoured his own children; having overthrown his own father, he was determined to avoid the same fate.
The face of Saturn, his eyes popping out of their sockets, is a mask of hate and cruelty; few artists have ever painted anything so horrible.

17. GOYA'S LIFE ♦ *In 1815 Goya was almost seventy. He had a new companion, a young woman named Leocadia Weiss, but it was a difficult year: he seems to have felt sidelined, although he was readmitted to court after an inquiry concluded that he had not collaborated with the French. Despite his poor health, Goya continued to work prodigiously. 1816 was devoted to etching, and he published a series of 33 plates dedicated to bullfighting. After a visit to Andalusia, he returned to Madrid and purchased the house known as the "Quinta del Sordo." He was commissioned to execute what was to be his last religious painting,* The Last Communion of St. Joseph of Calasanz. ⇒♦

BULLFIGHTING

For centuries Spain existed in semi-isolation, thanks partly to historical accidents and partly to its geography: the Pyrenees acted as a formidable barrier to new ideas. Meanwhile the Spanish people became deeply attached to the country's traditions, one of the most enduring of which was the bullfight, the *corrida*. This spectacle became a passion that united all social classes; it was a source of joy and sorrow, the subject of endless arguments, and the stuff of dreams. The *corrida* offered a contest of strength, honor, and skill, played out before eager crowds in a festive atmosphere. From his childhood, Goya, a true Spaniard, loved the *corrida*. He painted a number of scenes with matadors and bulls, and, in 1816, he published *La Tauromaquia*, a set of 33 etchings about bullfighting. He returned to the subject again after settling in the South of France, where there were also arenas, using the still-novel technique of lithography to create the *Bulls of Bordeaux* series (1825).

♦ A SPANISH PASSION
In 1799, when he was just over 30, Goya painted a tapestry cartoon called the *Novillada*, of which the above is a detail (Prado, Madrid).
"Four boys are amusing themselves; one brings the bull into the enclosure, another makes a pass with the cloak, while the others look on."
This is how Goya described the scene, perhaps portraying himself in the strong, energetic boy grappling with the young bull.
The bullfight and its protagonists crop up again and again in Goya's work: portraits of bullfighters, scenes of fiestas, individuals, and episodes from bullfights.
He used a variety of techniques: paintings on canvas and on metal, drawings, and etchings.
The most closely related group of pictures is the *Tauromaquia*, a series of etchings that were put on sale in 1816 by an art dealer in Madrid.
In Bordeaux, thanks to his friendship with a printer, Cyprien Gaulon, Goya experimented with a new medium for making prints: lithography, which he had already tried in Madrid without much success.
The result was the group of four splendid plates known as *The Bulls of Bordeaux*.

♦ THE FAMOUS AMERICAN MARIANO CEBALLOS
The main figure in this lithograph, drawn from memory, is the famous "El Indio," whose nickname alluded to his Native American origin. El Indio's specialty was to perform, as here, mounted on a bull. It is the final moment of the contest, when he is about to strike. The bullfighter, the incarnation of macho values, is still the Spanish national hero.

The means used to create this masterpiece were simple: some crayons, a scraper, and a razor. The drawing was done on a lithographic stone, which was then used to print onto paper. Nevertheless, Goya was able to create effects of light and movement, and succeeded in conveying the sense of excitement and energy so typical of *the struggle in the arena. The white of the bull's back, the dark masses of audience and participants, and the shadows cast by the combatants give the scene an intensely dramatic quality. Goya's works demonstrated the possibilities of lithography, a technique that would be taken up by later painters from the Impressionists to Picasso.*

1

2

3

4

5

6

7

♦ **An inexhaustible source of inspiration**
Goya portrayed the most important maneuvers and the crucial moments of the bullfight. He had always been fascinated by bullfighting and, as a young man, he had taken part personally in a bullfight. In Spain bullfighting became a popular cult, above all in the second half of the 18th century, when many arenas were built and codes and regulations were formulated. The origin of bullfighting was also debated: was it Muslim or Christian? Figures 1 and 2 above are part of a series entitled *Amusements in Spain*. The others belong to the 1816 collection of etchings entitled *La Tauromaquia*:
3. *The Agility and Bravery of Juanito Apiñani in the Arena of Madrid.*
4. *Unleashing the Dogs Against the Bull.*
5. *The Unfortunate Death of Pepe Illo in the Madrid Arena.*
6. *Ceballos Himself, Riding a Bull, Breaks Short Spears in the Madrid Arena.*
7. *Banderillas with Fire-darts.*

GOYA IN PARIS

In 1824, when Goya visited Paris, the French capital had long been at the center of European culture, fashion, and art. French police files noted that the elderly Spanish painter spent much of his time going to museums. For the culturally aware tourist, a visit to the Louvre was obligatory. This famous museum housed a magnificent permanent collection, and was also where "the Salon" was held – an annual exhibition of what were considered to be the finest works of art currently being produced. The Salon was the only place where a painter could make a great public reputation, and a new movement could hope to establish itself. The artists who made the greatest impact in 1824 were the French Romantic Delacroix and the British landscapist Constable. Goya no doubt admired the works by them that were on show, but it is unlikely that they influenced him. In Paris, the Spanish community welcomed him with respect, but neither Goya nor his art were as yet known in France.

♦ SALON VISITORS
The Salon was a fashionable as well as a cultural event, attracting many visitors. The awarding of prizes and honorable mentions was followed by a public that was generally rather conformist in taste.

In 1824, the Salon
Carré of the Louvre
exhibited many works
by important artists,
including Delacroix,
a very controversial
figure. Goya, who was
deaf and frail and did
not speak French,
visited the Salon with
a cousin of his
daughter-in-law,
Jeronimo Goicoechea.
These were the early
days of his exile and
all his movements
were closely watched
by the police.

♦ THE MASSACRE
OF CHIOS
Delacroix, 1824;
Louvre, Paris. This
work was severely
criticized for the bold
colors and exotic
violence with which
Delacroix described
an episode in the war
of independence being
waged by the Greeks
against the Turks.
Delacroix had
attracted notice at
the Salon of 1822,
with his dramatic
Dante and Virgil.

♦ THE HAY WAIN
Constable, 1821;
National Gallery,
London. This English
landscape and other
works by John
Constable enjoyed
great success at the
1824 Salon. The
leading French
painter of the day,
Delacroix, was
influenced by
Constable, as, later,
were the painters of
the Barbizon School
and other pioneering
landscapists.

18. GOYA'S LIFE ♦ *Another serious illness brought Goya
close to death, but he was carefully looked after and
managed to recover. In 1820 another political upheaval
led to the granting of a liberal constitution, but three years
later the reactionary Ferdinand VII was back in control.
Goya gave his house, the "Quinta del Sordo," to his
grandson, Mariano, and prepared to go into voluntary
exile. He left Spain in 1824, on the pretext of seeking
treatment at a spa, and, after a visit to Paris, he moved to
Bordeaux, where Leocadia joined him. He adopted a new
technique, painting miniatures on ivory, and made a set
of lithographs,* The Bulls of Bordeaux. ➡

THE MILKMAID OF BORDEAUX

Goya's last masterpiece was the portrait of a girl he saw passing his window every morning on a donkey that took her into town from the countryside. The work is like a gesture of farewell, filled with a radiant tenderness. The period of the "black paintings" was over. Despite his precarious health, Goya now worked "furiously," his friend Moratín related, but with more tranquillity. He never stopped experimenting: during his French exile he painted a group of miniatures on ivory, and on a drawing of 1824–25 he wrote "*Aun aprendo*" (I am still learning). *The Milkmaid of Bordeaux* has often been called a "pre-Impressionist" work, referring to the French art movement of the 1870s. Even though it was painted half a century before Monet, Renoir, and other Impressionists came to the fore, Goya's work has similar characteristics, using rapid, free brushwork to capture the light and atmosphere of a scene, in a way impossible when using a more laborious technique.

♦ **OFFICIAL PORTRAIT** When Goya visited Madrid in 1826, the court painter Vicente López was given the task of painting his portrait. It is believed that Goya made some small modifications and insisted that López should stop painting only when Goya judged the work to be finished.

♦ **THE WORK** *The Milkmaid of Bordeaux*, 1827; oil on canvas, 29 x 27 in (74 x 68 cm); Prado, Madrid. At the age of 80, after a final journey to Madrid, Goya returned to Bordeaux and set to work as usual. His life was tranquil enough with Leocadia and her children, especially the young Rosaria, a girl, perhaps even his own daughter, whom Goya loved dearly. When she was only seven, Goya gave her drawing and painting lessons. She was exceptionally gifted and some sketches were done jointly with Goya himself. Goya executed *The Milkmaid of Bordeaux* rapidly, almost in a single session. His friend Moratín said that in this period Goya never corrected his work or changed his mind, such was the confidence he had acquired and maintained until the end. Goya died the following year, 1828. Leocadia Weiss kept *The Milkmaid*, but not for long: unprovided for by Goya and short of money, she sold it to Don Juan de Muguiro, a relative by marriage of Javier Goya. Muguiro had been a friend of the artist, who had painted his portrait in 1827. How much Muguiro paid for *The Milkmaid* is not known. Goya advised Leocadia not to sell it for less than an ounce of gold, so he was aware of its quality. Above: Leandro Fernandez Moratín, 1824; Museo de Bellas Artes, Bilbao.

The light enveloping the figure falls on the bonnet and shawl, suffusing the materials so that they glow and gleam. The freely painted background creates an impalpable atmosphere that contrasts with the solidity of the seated woman. The vibrant light, the dabs of color, and the short, urgent brushstrokes, soft and almost caressing, anticipate the technique of the Impressionists.

♦ **THE PROFILE OF THE MILKMAID** Under the dark hair, there is a fresh, youthful, tender face, with a bright complexion and a hint of melancholy in the expression. In her naturalness, the girl can be seen as a symbol of youth and untainted life. Goya's noble and royal models are now a distant memory.

♦ **MAN EATING LEEKS**
Once he reached maturity, Goya never imitated any artist. Even as a miniaturist he was entirely original. He blackened the ivory plaque, then allowed a drop of water to fall on it and spread out. In the clear areas which were arbitrarily created in this fashion, Goya painted the images they suggested to him.

♦ **OLD MAN ON A SWING**
This charcoal drawing from 1824–28 shows an old man amusing himself as if he were a child. It represents an innocent impulse with which Goya seems to sympathize.

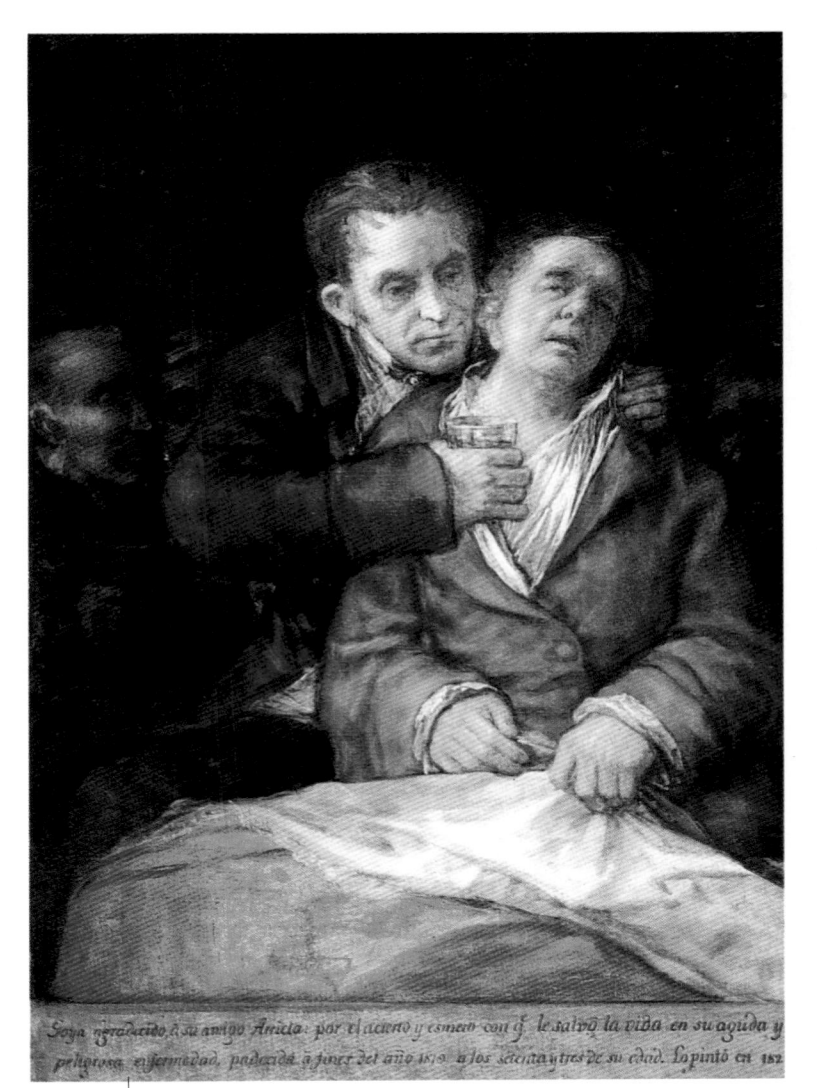

♦ **SELF-PORTRAIT WITH DR. ARRIETA**
1820; Art Institute, Minneapolis. In 1819, Goya suffered a short but painful illness, of which he was cured with great skill and devotion by Dr. Arrieta. Goya painted this scene to show his gratitude. Though his health had given him problems for at least 30 years, they never broke his resistance.

♦ **MAN PICKING FLEAS FROM A DOG**
A miniature painted on an ivory plaque. To economize on his use of precious ivory, Goya wiped clean many plaques in order to reuse them. In all he painted about 40, declaring himself very satisfied with them. Both this and the miniature *Man Eating Leeks* (above left) are now in the Staatliche Kunstsammlungen, Dresden.

THE PRADO

More than half of Goya's vast artistic production is in Madrid, in churches, private collections, palaces, and museums. The Prado is particularly rich, and is the best place to go to become acquainted with Goya. More than a fifth of his paintings and a large selection of his drawings and etchings are housed in the museum. The monumental building was erected in 1811–19, to designs by the architect Juan de Villanueva. Its purpose was to hold the Spanish royal collections: art treasures that had belonged to Isabella of Castille, Charles V, Philip II, and Philip IV, including masterpieces from all the major European schools. Italian and Flemish artists are splendidly represented, but by far the greatest body of work is that of Spanish artists – Velázquez, El Greco, Murillo, Ribera, Zurbarán, and, of course, Goya. Goya's life and artistic career are superbly displayed in the rooms of the Prado, providing the interested visitor with an enthralling experience.

♦ THE CREATION OF THE PRADO
The idea that an artistic heritage should be made available to everybody was established in the 18th century. The popes were among the first to open their collections to the public: the Capitoline Museum in Rome was founded in 1734. In 1759 the nucleus of the British Museum was opened in London, and in 1769 the collection of the Uffizi was entrusted to the city of Florence by Grand-Duke Pietro Leopoldo. In 1793 the French National Assembly transformed the royal collections of the Louvre in Paris into the Musée Central des Arts. During the Napoleonic period the museum held works of art looted from defeated countries, and so the Louvre became at once a celebratory image of the nation and a symbol of the universality of art and culture. The French model was soon exported and new museums were founded, among them the Prado. In 1808 Joseph Bonaparte, then King of Spain, ordered the creation of a museum to house the works of art confiscated from churches, convents, and private owners. The project was carried out by Ferdinand VII, during the Restoration. He added the royal collections and had built the great Neoclassical palace, inaugurated in 1819, which still houses the greatest museum in Spain.

♦ THE GOYA ROOMS
The Goya rooms at the Prado house an extraordinary selection of his works: from *Christ on the Cross*, a youthful work painted to gain admission into the Academy, to the achievements of his maturity: portraits, "black paintings," the *Caprichos*, *The Disasters of War*, and *The Milkmaid of Bordeaux*.

THE GOYA DOOR ♦
One entrance to the Prado is dedicated to Goya. The other two are dedicated to Velázquez and Murillo.

THE ROOMS ON ♦ THE GROUND FLOOR
These rooms contain the "black paintings," arranged in the same way as they were laid out by Goya in the House of the Deaf Man.

♦ WITCHES' SABBATH
1821–23.
Also known as *The Great He-Goat*, this work returns to a subject that Goya had painted 25 years before. The version here, far more sinister and terrifying, is one of the "black paintings."

19. GOYA'S LIFE ♦ *In 1826 Goya was still in reasonable health, and he decided to undertake a journey to Spain to obtain funds for his retirement. The king granted him an annuity of 50,000 reals. Soon afterward he returned to Bordeaux, where he was happy and where he painted his last masterpiece: a pensive and humble milkmaid who passed by his window every morning. In 1827 he went to Madrid for the last time, to see his beloved grandchild Mariano and execute a splendid portrait of him. The following year Goya fell ill. He died on April 16, 1828, at the age of 80.* ▶

♦ THE SECOND OF MAY 1808: CHARGE OF THE MAMELUKES 1814. This is the initial episode of the Spanish insurrection against the French army. Legend has it that Goya witnessed the bloody scene at the Puerta del Sol in Madrid and made a sketch of it from life. However, the painting is certainly not literally accurate.

♦ THE ROOMS ON THE FIRST FLOOR An entire wing of the Prado is dedicated to Goya. It houses a considerable part of his life's production, including his tapestry cartoons and most famous etchings.

♦ THE DUKE AND DUCHESS OF OSUNA WITH THEIR CHILDREN 1788. The duke and duchess were enlightened and enthusiastic patrons of Goya. He had also painted separate portraits of them in 1785.

♦ SELF-PORTRAIT AT THE AGE OF 69 1815. Another version of this painting at the Prado is kept at the Academy of San Fernando. The small self-portrait (18 x 14 in: 46 x 35 cm) shows a worn-looking Goya. His eyes are intense but surrounded by dark circles, suggesting the strains and stresses he knew in his old age.

♦ KEY DATES IN GOYA'S LIFE

1746 On March 30, Francisco Goya y Lucientes, the sixth son of a gilder, Juan Goya, is born at Fuendetodos, near Saragossa.

1760 He gains his first experience of painting in the studio of José Luzán, an artist of modest reputation, with whom he studies reproductions of the great masters.

1763 He takes part in the competition for admission to the Royal Academy of Fine Arts of San Fernando in Madrid, but is rejected; this happens again in 1766.

1770 Goya travels to Italy and visits Rome, where he stays for more than a year. He takes part in a competition held by the Academy of Parma.

1772 His first main commission is to decorate a chapel in the Cathedral of Saragossa. In 1773 he marries Josefa Bayeu, sister of fashionable painter Francisco Bayeu.

1774 In Madrid, Mengs, the Court Painter, commissions Goya to paint cartoons for tapestries to be made at the factory of Santa Barbara.

1780 Goya is unanimously elected a member of the Royal Academy of Fine Arts of San Fernando and meets the statesman and writer Jovellanos.

1786 Goya is appointed Painter to the King and three years later Court Painter of Charles IV – a position representing the high point in a court artist's career.

1792 He makes a journey to Andalusia. Later, in Cadiz, he is struck down by a serious illness. He eventually recovers, but is left permanently deaf.

1796 He stays with the Duchess of Alba in Andalusia, and possibly has a love affair with her. He paints several portraits of her.

1799 Goya publishes *Los Caprichos*, a group of 80 satirical etchings which are almost immediately withdrawn as a result of the pressure applied by the Inquisition.

1800 He paints a famous portrait of the royal family and in the following years establishes a reputation as the most fashionable portraitist of the Spanish nobility.

1810 Goya's personal experience of the war against the French is intensely felt, and in 1814 inspires famous paintings such as *The Third of May*.

1816 Now remote from the court and its influence, Goya makes a series of etchings, *The Disasters of War*, and publishes 35 bullfighting plates, the *Tauromaquia*.

1818 Goya buys the House of the Deaf Man, in which he paints directly on the walls the terrible, visionary "black paintings." He continues to work as an etcher, tackling a variety of subjects.

1824 Using his health as a pretext, he leaves for Bordeaux, to which he moves with Leocadia Weiss, his young companion, after a brief visit to Paris. In 1825 he makes a set of lithographs, *The Bulls of Bordeaux*.

1828 *The Milkmaid of Bordeaux* (1827) is Goya's final masterpiece. Goya dies on April 16, 1828.

♦ WHERE TO SEE WORKS BY GOYA

SPAIN

MADRID. The Prado houses more than 150 of Goya's works (not including drawings), most of which are incontestably masterpieces. Among them are cartoons for tapestries: *The Parasol, The Washerwoman, The Swing, The Meadow of St. Isidore*. Even more famous are paintings such as *The Second of May, The Third of May, The Giant, The Family of Charles IV*, wonderful *neral Antonio Ricardos*, still-life paintings including *Dead Turkey*, the fabulous *Clothed* and *Naked Majas*, and the late *Milkmaid of Bordeaux*. No other museum can boast such dramatic examples of artistic reportage and mental turmoil as the rooms in the Prado showing *The Disasters of War* and the forty "black paintings" (*Saturn, Asmodea, Leocadia*, etc.), which were detached from the walls of the House of the Deaf Man where Goya lived.
At the Lázaro Galdiano Museum there are cartoons for tapestries including *The Harvest*, cartoons for frescoes, and such paintings as *The Witches' Sabbath* and the portrait of *The Count of Miranda*. Among the pictures to be seen at the Royal Academy of San Fernando are *The Burial of the Sardine, A Procession of Flagellants*, and *Inquisition Scene*. The splendid portraits in the Academy include *Manuel Godoy on the Field of Battle* and *The Tyrant*, and there is also a well-known self-portrait of 1815. The most important Goyas in the Royal Palace are the official portraits of King Charles IV and Queen María Luisa. The Museo Thyssen-Bornemisza has Goya's highly original portrait of a blind beggar-guitarist, *Tío Paquete*. And perhaps his finest religious frescoes are in the Church of San Antonio de la Florida.
SARAGOSSA. As well as the frescoes in the cathedral of El Pilar, there are seven mural paintings (1774), damaged in an earthquake but restored, in the Aula Dei; they illustrate episodes in the lives of the Virgin and Christ. At the Museum of Saragossa, the most significant works are the *Portrait of Ferdinand VII, Apparition of the Virgin of the Pillar*, and the striking *Portrait of a Man*, possibly a self-portrait, though some experts believe it is not by Goya.

FRANCE

PARIS. In the Louvre are three portraits by Goya, including the *Marquesa de la Solana*, and the still-life *Counter of the Butcher's Shop*. The Bibliothèque Nationale houses a version of *Majas on a Balcony* and some *Tauromaquia* lithographs. Goya is even better represented in French provincial museums. A museum devoted to his work at CASTRES has paintings such as *The Assembly of the Company of the Philippines* and the *Self-portrait with Spectacles*. In the museum at AGEN are *Ascension in a Montgolfier Balloon* and the 1783 *Self-portrait*. The museum of BAYONNE houses the *Portait of the Duke of Osuna*, while the Musée des Beaux-Arts, LILLE, has *The Old Women* and *The Letter* (or *The Young Women*).

GREAT BRITAIN

LONDON. Works by Goya at the National Gallery include portraits of the Duke of Wellington and Isabel de Porcel and *The Forcibly Bewitched* (1798). At the Wellington Museum, Apsley House, there is an equestrian portrait of the Duke. In OXFORD, the Ashmolean Museum holds two bullfighting scenes The National Gallery, EDINBURGH, exhibits a cartoon for a tapestry, *The Doctor*, while Pollock House, GLASGOW, has one of the *Boys Playing* series. In DUBLIN, the National Gallery of Ireland has a work of 1790, *The Dream*.

USA AND CANADA

There are about 100 Goyas in the USA. In WASHINGTON, D.C., the portraits of Bartolomé Sureda and his wife, and *Young Woman with a Fan*, are at the National Gallery. The Metropolitan Museum, NEW YORK, has the doubtfully attributed *Majas on a Balcony* and portraits such as *Manuel Osorio Manrique de Zuñiga* (1788) and *Pepito Costa y Bonells*. *The Duchess of Alba* (1797) also hangs in New York, at the Hispanic Society of America. At the Art Institute of CHICAGO are six small paintings in which Goya pictured the capture of a notorious bandit, El Maragato (1807).The MINNEAPOLIS Art Institute contains *Self-portrait with Dr. Arrieta*. Canada's MONTREAL Museum has three portraits.

GERMANY

MUNICH. One of the finest of Goya's still-lifes, *Plucked Turkey* (1810), hangs in the Alte Pinakothek. In FRANKFURT the Städelsches Kunstinstitut shows two of *The Disasters of War*. Other works can be found in DRESDEN, BERLIN, KARLSRUHE, and HAMBURG.

ITALY

PARMA has one of Goya's masterpieces, *The Family of Don Luis*, which is held by the Magnani Rocca Foundation. The Uffizi in FLORENCE exhibits *The Matador Pedro Romero, The Countess of Chinchón*, and an equestrian portrait of María Teresa Vallabriga. There is a *Procession* at the Brera, MILAN, while at NAPLES the Museo di Capodimonte has portraits of Charles IV and María Luisa.

SWITZERLAND

The BASEL Museum possesses a preliminary sketch for one of the "black paintings" (*Fantastic Vision*, 1819). In the Bührle Collection, ZURICH, there are two pictures of *Boys Playing* and *Procession at Valencia*. The Reinhart Foundation, WINTERTHUR, has still-lifes by Goya and the unfinished *Portrait of José Pío de Molina*.

♦ LIST OF WORKS INCLUDED IN THIS BOOK

The works reproduced in this book are listed here, with (when known) their date , their dimensions, the place where they are currently housed, and the page number. The letter E after the page number denotes that the work is reproduced in its entirety. The letter D indicates that only a detail is shown. The numbers in bold type refer to the credits on page 64.

ANONYMOUS
1. *Frederick II of Prussia and Voltaire,* 19th century, colored lithograph, 22 D
2. *Portrait of Louis XVI,* 18th century, oil on canvas, 33 D
CANOVA, ANTONIO (1757–1822)
3. *Cupid Waking Psyche with a Kiss,* 1787–93, marble, 155 x 168 cm (Louvre, Paris) 39 E; **4.** *Paoline Borghese as Venus,* 1804–8, marble, length 200 cm (Galleria Borghese, Rome) 38 D
CARAVAGGIO (MICHELANGELO MERISI CALLED, 1573–1610)
5. *The Calling of St. Matthew,* 1599–1600, oil on canvas (San Luigi dei Francesi, Rome) 11 E
CONSTABLE, JOHN (1776–1837)
6. *The Hay Wain,* 1821, oil on canvas, 130.5 x 185.5 cm (National Gallery, London) 57 E; **7.** *Trees at Hampstead,* 1821, oil on canvas, 91.5 x 72.5 cm (Victoria and Albert Museum, London) 38 D
CRESPI, GIUSEPPE MARIA, CALLED "LO SPAGNUOLO" (1665–1747)
8. *The Confirmation,* c. 1740 (Gemäldegalerie, Dresden) 12 D
DAVID, JACQUES-LOUIS (1748–1825)
9. *The Death of Marat,* 1793, oil on canvas (Musées Royaux des Beaux Arts, Brussels) 32 E; **10.** *Napoleon Crossing the Alps,* 1801, oil on canvas (Musée National du Château de Malmaison, Rueil) 38 E; **11.** *The Sabine Women,* 1799, oil on canvas, 386 x 520 cm (Louvre, Paris) 39 E
DELACROIX, EUGENE (1798–1863)
12. *Liberty Leading the People,* 1830, oil on canvas, 260 x 325 cm (Louvre, Paris) 33 E; **13.** *The Massacre of Chios,* 1824, oil on canvas, 417 x 354 cm (Louvre, Paris) 57 E
FRIEDRICH, CASPAR DAVID (1774–1840)
14. *Abbey in the Oak Wood,* 1809–10, oil on canvas, 109 x 170 cm (Staatliche Museen, Berlin) 39 E
FUSELI, JOHANN HEINRICH (1741–1825)
15. *The Nightmare,* 1781, oil on canvas, 101.6 x 127 cm (Bibliothèque Nationale, Paris) 28 D; **16.** *Reclining Nude and Piano Player,* 1799–1800, oil on canvas, 71 x 91 cm (Offentliche Kunstsammlung, Basel) 40 E
GÉRICAULT, THÉODORE (1791–1824)
17. *The Raft of the "Medusa",* 1819, oil on canvas, 491 x 716 cm (Louvre, Paris) 39 E
GIAQUINTO, CORRADO (1703–66)
18. *The Adoration of the Name of God,* 1741–43, fresco (Santa Croce in Jerusalem, Rome) 14 E
GOYA, FRANCISCO (1746–1828)
19. *The Adoration of the Name of God by Angels,* 1772, fresco, 7 x 15 m (Saragossa cathedral) 12 E; **20.** *The Adoration of the Name of God by Angels,* 1772, oil on canvas, 75 x 152 cm (Gudiol, Barcelona) 12 D; **21.** *Against the Common Good,* 1815–20, etching, 175 x 220, D; **22.** *Against Convention,* etching (Prado, Madrid) 37 E; **23.** *The Agility and Bravery of Juanito Apiñani in the Arena of Madrid,* 1815, etching, 24.5 x 35.5 cm (*Tauromaquia* series) 55 E; **24.** *Amusements in Spain,* 1825, lithograph, 25.5 x 35 cm (Prado, Madrid) 55 E, D; **25.** *Ascension in a Montgolfier Balloon,* 1813–15, oil on canvas, 103 x 83 cm (Musée, Agen) 50 D; **26.** *Asmodea,* 1820–21, oil on wall then on canvas, 123 x 265 cm (Prado, Madrid) 52 E, D; **27.** *Banderillas with Fire-darts,* 1812, etching, 25.5 x 35 cm (*Tauromaquia* series) 55 E; **28.** *Boys with Mastiffs,* 1786–87, oil on canvas, 112 x 145 cm (Prado, Madrid) 30 E, D; **29.** *The Burial of Christ,* 1771, oil on wall then on canvas, 130 x 95 cm (Lázaro Galdiano Museum, Madrid) 13 E; **30.** *The Burial of the Sardine,* 1812–14, oil on canvas, 82.5 x 52 cm (Academy of San Fernando, Madrid) 51 E, D; **31.** *The Carnivorous Vulture,* 1810–20, etching, 175 x 220 cm (Academy of San Fernando, Madrid) 49 E; **32.** *Ceballos Himself, Riding a Bull, Breaks Short Spears in the Madrid Arena,* 1815, etching, 24.5 x 35.5 cm (Prado, Madrid) 55 E; **33.** *Charles III in the Guise of a Hunter,* 1786–88, oil on canvas, 210 x 127 cm (private collection, Madrid) 22 E; **34.** *Charles IV on Horseback,* 1799, oil on canvas, 305 x 279 cm (Prado, Madrid) 27 E; *Christ on the Cross,* 1780, oil on canvas, 255 x 153 cm (Prado, Madrid) 15 E, D; **37.** *The Circumcision,* 1774, oil on wall, 305 x 1025 cm (Aula Dei, Saragossa) 13 D; **38.** *The City on a Rock,* 1813–16, oil on canvas, 84 x 104 cm (Metropolitan Museum, New York) 51 E; **39.** *The Clothed Maja,* 1805, oil on canvas, 95 x 190 cm (Prado, Madrid) 40 E, D; **40.** *Count Fernan Nuñez,* 1803, oil on canvas, 211 x 137 cm (private collection, Madrid) 43 E; **41.** *Count Francisco Cabarrús,* 1786–87, oil on canvas, 210 x 127 cm (Banco de España, Madrid) 23 E; **42.** *The Countess of Chinchón,* 1800, oil on canvas, 216 x 144 cm (De Sueca, Madrid) 25 E; **43.** *The Crockery Vendor,* 1778, oil on canvas, 259 x 220 cm (Prado, Madrid) 16 E; **44.** *Dog,* 1820–21, oil on wall then on canvas, 134 x 80 cm (Prado, Madrid) 52 E, D; **45.** *Don Pantaleón Pérez de Nenin,* 1808, oil on canvas, 206 x 125 cm (Banco Exterior, Madrid) 43 E; **46.** *The Dream of Joseph,* 1771, oil on wall then on canvas, 130 x 95.5 cm (Museo de Bellas Artes, Saragossa) 13 E, D; **47.** *The Duchess of Alba,* 1795, oil on canvas, 194 x 130 cm (De Alba, Madrid) 36 E; **48.** *The Duchess of Alba,* 1797, oil on canvas, 210 x 149.5 cm (Hispanic Society, New York) 36 E; **49.** *The Duchess of Alba Arranges her Hair,* 1796–97 (Biblioteca Nacional, Madrid) 37 E; **50.** *The Duchess with her Chaperone,* 1795, oil on canvas, 194 x 130 cm (Prado, Madrid) 37 E, D; **51.** *The Duke and Duchess of Osuna with their Children,* 1788, oil on canvas, 225 x 174 cm (Prado, Madrid) 61 E; **52.** *The Family of Charles IV,* 1801, oil on canvas, 280 x 336 cm (Prado, Madrid) 34 E, D; **53.** *The Family of the Infante Don Luis,* 1783, oil on canvas, 248 x 330 cm (Magnani Rocca Foundation) 24 E, D; **54.** *The Famous American Mariano Ceballos,* 1825, lithograph, 24.5 x 35 cm (Prado, Madrid) 54 E, D; **55.** *For a Knife,* 1810–20, etching, 15.5 x 20.5 cm (Academy of San Fernando, Madrid) 48 D; **56.** *Francisca Sabasa y Garcia,* 1808, oil on canvas, 71 x 58 cm (National Gallery, Washington, D.C.) 43 E; **57.** *Gaspar Melchor de Jovellanos y Ramirez,* 1785, oil on canvas, 185 x 110 cm (Valls y Taberner, Barcelona) 26 E; **58.** *General Antonio Ricardos,* 1793–94, oil on canvas, 112 x 84 cm (Prado, Madrid) 33 E; **59.** *The Giant,* 1808–12, oil on canvas, 116 x 105 cm (Prado, Madrid) 50 E, D; **60.** *The Giant,* 1810–18, oil on canvas (Bibliothèque Nationale, Paris) 51 E; **61.** *God Forgive Her, She Was Her Mother,* 1799, etching, 21 x 15 cm (*Los Caprichos* series) 28 E; **62.** *Hannibal Looks Upon Italy from the Alps,* 1770–71, oil on canvas (private collection) 10 E; **63.** *The Hermitage of St. Isidore,* 1788, oil on canvas, 42 x 44 cm (Prado, Madrid) 18 D; **64.** *A Heroic Feat! With Dead Men!,* 1810–20, etching, 15.5 x 20.5 cm (Academy of San Fernando, Madrid) 48 E; **65.** *The Infante Francisco de Paula Antonio,* 1800, oil on canvas, 74 x 60 cm (Prado, Madrid) 31 E; **66.** *Isabel de Porcel,* 1804–5, oil on canvas, 81 x 54 cm (National Gallery, London) 42 E, D; **67.** *Josefa Bayeu de Goya,* 1795–96, oil on canvas, 81 x 56 cm (Prado, Madrid) 11 E; **68.** *José Moñino, Count of Floridablanca, with Goya and the Architect Sabatini,* 1783, oil on canvas, 262 x 166 cm (Banco Urquijo, Madrid) 22 E; **69.** *The Kite,* 1778, oil on canvas, 269 x 285 cm (Prado, Madrid) 21 E; **70.** *Leandro Fernandez de Moratín,* 1824, oil on canvas, 60 x 49.5 cm (Museo de Bellas Artes, Bilbao) 58 D; **71.** *Leocadia,* 1821–23, oil on wall then on canvas, 147 x 1 32 cm (Prado, Madrid) 53 E; **72.** *The Madonna of the Pillar,* c. 1770, oil on canvas, 78 x 52 cm (Museo de Bellas Artes, Saragossa) 7 E; **73.** *Majas on a Balcony,* 1808–12, oil on canvas, 195 x 125.5 cm (Metropolitan Museum, New York) 49 E; **74.** *Man Eating Leeks,* 1825, miniature on ivory, 6.2 x 5.6 cm (Kupferstichkabinett, Staatliche Kunstsammlungen, Dresden) 59 E; **75.** *Man Picking Fleas from a Dog,* 1825, miniature on ivory, 8.8 x 8.6 cm (Kupferstichkabinett, Staatliche Kunstsammlungen, Dresden) 59 E; **76.** *Manuel Godoy on the Field of Battle,* 1801, oil on canvas, 181 x 268 cm (Academy of San Fernando, Madrid) 44 D; **77.** *Manuel Osorio de Manrique Zuñiga,* 1788, oil on canvas, 127 x 106 cm (Metropolitan Museum, New York) 31 E; **78.** *Maria Ana de Pontejos y Sandoval,* 1786, oil on canvas, 211.5 x 126 cm (National Gallery, Washington, D.C.) 42 E; **79.** *María Luisa on Horseback,* 1799, oil on canvas, 335 x 279 cm (Prado, Madrid) 27 E; **80.** *Mariano Goya,* 1813–15, oil on canvas, 59 x 47 cm (Prado, Madrid) 31 E; **81.** *The Marquesa de la Solana,* 1794–95, oil on canvas, 181 x 122 cm (Louvre, Paris) 43 E; **82.** *Mary, Queen of Martyrs,* 1780–81, fresco (Saragossa cathedral) 21 E; **83.** *The Matador Pedro Romero,* 1795–98, oil on canvas, 84 x 65 cm (Kimbell Art Museum, Fortworth) 37 D; **84.** *May The Rope Break!,* 1810–20, etching, 175 x 220 cm (Academy of San Fernando, Madrid) 49 E; **85.** *The Meadow of St. Isidore,* 1788, oil on canvas, 44 x 94 cm (Prado, Madrid) 18 E, D; **86.** *The Milkmaid of Bordeaux,* 1827, oil on canvas, 74 x 68 cm (Prado, Madrid) 58 E, D; **87.** *The Miracle of St. Anthony of Padua,* 1798, fresco, diameter 520 cm (San Antonio de la Florida, Manzanares) 35 E, D; **88.** *The Naked Maja,* 1800, oil on canvas, 97 x 190 cm (Prado, Madrid) 41 E, D; **89.** *The Novillada,* 1779, oil on canvas, 259 x 136 cm (Prado, Madrid) 54 D; **90.** *Old Man on a Swing,* 1824–28, charcoal (Hispanic Society, New York) 59 E; **91.** *The Parasol,* 1777, oil on canvas, 104 x 152 cm (Prado, Madrid) 17 E; **92.** *The Pilgrimage of St. Isidore,* 1821–23, oil on wall then on canvas, 140 x 438 cm (Prado, Madrid) 19 E, D; **93.** *Sacrifice to Priapus,* 1771, oil on canvas, 33 x 24 cm (Gudiol, Barcelona) 10 E; **94.** *Sad Presentiments of What is About to Happen,* 1810–20, etching, 15.5 x 20.5 cm (Prado, Madrid) 48 D; **95.** *Saturn,* 1821–23, oil on wall then on canvas, 146 x 83 cm (Prado, Madrid) 53 E, D; **96.** *The Second of May 1808: Charge of the Mamelukes,* 1814, oil on canvas, 266 x 345 cm (Prado, Madrid) 61 E; **97.** *Self-portrait,* 1795, china ink (Metropolitan Museum, New York) 37 E; **98.** *Self-portrait at the Age of 69,* 1815, oil on canvas, 46 x 35 cm (Prado, Madrid) 61 E; **99.** *Self-portrait with Dr. Arrieta,* 1820, oil on canvas, 115 x 79 cm (Art Institute, Minneapolis) 59 E; **100.** *The Sleep of Reason Produces Monsters,* 1799, etching, 21 x 15 cm (*Los Caprichos* series) 28 E; **101.** *Spanish Rebels Making Bullets,* 1812–13, oil on wood, 33 x 52 cm (Palacio Real, Madrid) 44 E; **102.** *Spanish Rebels Making Gunpowder,* 1812–13, oil on wood, 33 x 52 cm (Palacio Real, Madrid) 45 E; **103.** *St. Bernardine of Siena Preaching to King Alfonso V of Aragon,* 1782–83, oil on canvas, 48 x 300 cm (San Francisco el Grande, Madrid) 20 E, D; **104.** *Standing self-portrait,* 1793–95, oil on canvas, 42 x 28 cm (private collection, Madrid) 26 E; **105.** *They Already Have a Seat,* 1799, etching, 21 x 15 cm (*Los Caprichos* series) 29 E; **106.** *The Third of May 1808,* 1814, oil on canvas, 266 x 345 cm (Prado, Madrid) 46 E, D; **107.** *This is Worse,* 1810–20, etching, 15.5 x 20.5 cm (Academy of San Fernando, Madrid) 48 E; **108.** *Two Old Men,* 1821–24, oil on wall then on canvas, 144 x 66 cm (Prado, Madrid) 53 D; **109.** *The Tyrant,* 1799, oil on canvas, 206.5 x 130.5 cm (Academy of San Fernando, Madrid) 33 E; **110.** *The Unfortunate Death of Pepe Illo in the Madrid Arena,* 1815, etching, 24.5 x 35.5 cm (Prado, Madrid) 55 E; **111.** *Unleashing the Dogs Against the Bull,* 1815, etching, 24.5 x 35.5 cm (Prado, Madrid) 55 E; **112.** *The Wedding,* 1791, oil on canvas, 267 x 346 cm (Prado, Madrid) 31 D; **113.** *What Courage!* 1810–20, etching, 15.5 x 21 cm (Academy of San Fernando, Madrid) 49 E; **114.** *What Worse Thing Could Be Done?,* 1810–20, etching, 15.5 x 20.5 cm (Academy of San Fernando, Madrid) 48 E; **115.** *Why?,* 1810–20, etching, 15.5 x 20.5 cm (Academy of San Fernando, Madrid) 48 E; **116.** *The Witches' Sabbath,* 1797–98, oil on canvas, 44 x 31 cm (Lázaro Galdiano Museum, Madrid) 29 D; **117.** *The Witches' Sabbath,* 1821–23, oil on wall then on canvas, 140 x 438 cm (Prado, Madrid) 60 E; **118.** *Young Woman with a Fan,* 1805–6, oil on canvas, 110 x 78 cm (National Gallery, Washington, D.C.) 42 E
LAMPI, GIOVANNI BATTISTA LAMPI THE ELDER (1751–1830)
119. *Catherine II of Russia,* 1794, oil on canvas, 230 x 162 cm (State Museum of Ethnography, Leningrad) 23 D
INGRES, JEAN-AUGUSTE-DOMINIQUE (1780–1867)
120. *The Bather of Valpinçon,* 1804, oil on canvas, 146 x 97.5 cm (Louvre, Paris) 39 E
KAUFMANN, ANGELICA (1741–1807)
121. *Johann Joachim Winckelmann,* 1764, oil on canvas (Kunsthaus, Zurich) 10 D
LOPEZ, VICENTE (1772–1850)
122 *Francisco Goya,* 1826, oil on canvas, 93 x 77 cm (Prado, Madrid) 58 E
LUZAN, JOSÉ MARTINEZ (1710-1785)
123. *Appearance of the Virgin of El Pilar,* 1764, oil on canvas (Our Lady of Cogulada, Saragossa) 14 E
MANET, EDOUARD (1832–83)
124. *Déjeuner sur l'herbe,* 1863, oil on canvas, 208 x 264.5 cm (Musée d'Orsay, Paris) 56 D; **125.** *The Execution of Maximilian of Mexico,* 1867, oil on canvas, 252 x 305 cm (Kunsthalle, Mannheim) 47 E, D; **126.** *Olympia,* 1863, oil on canvas, 130.5 x 190 cm (Musée d'Orsay, Paris) 41 E, D
MENGS, ANTON RAPHAEL (1728–79)
127. *Christ on the Cross,* 1761–69, oil on canvas (Prado, Madrid) 15 E; **128.** *Christ on the Cross,* 1761, preparatory sketch (Prado, Madrid) 15 D; **129.** *Self-portrait,* 1774, oil on canvas, 73.5 x 56 cm (Walker Art Gallery, Liverpool) 8 E
PIAZZETTA, GIOVANNI BATTISTA (1683–1754)
130. *The Ecstasy of St. Francis,* 1764, oil on canvas, 375 x 127 cm (Museo Civico, Vicenza) 12 D
PICASSO, PABLO (
131. *Massacre in Korea,* 1951, oil on canvas, 110 x 210 cm (Musée Picasso, Paris) 47 E;
REMBRANDT (1606–68)
132. *The Night Watch,* 1642, oil on canvas, 359 x 438 cm (Rijksmuseum, Amsterdam) 14 D; **133.** *Self-portrait at the Easel,* 1660, oil on canvas, 111 x 85 cm (Louvre, Paris) 14 D
ROBERT, HUBERT (1733–1808)
134. *Design for the Decoration of the Great Gallery of the Louvre,* 1796, oil on canvas (Louvre, Paris) 38 D
TIEPOLO, GIOVAN BATTISTA (1696-1770)
135. *Homage to the Emperor Frederick Barbarossa,* fresco (prince-bishop's residence, Würzburg) 8 D
TURNER, JOSEPH MALLORD WILLIAM (1793–1829)
136. *Buttermere Lake,* 1798, oil on canvas, 91.5 x 122 cm (Tate Gallery, London) 39 E
VELAZQUEZ, DIEGO (1599-1660)
137. *The Clown Sebastian de Morra,* c. 1644, oil on canvas, 106 x 81 cm (Prado, Madrid) 15 D; **138.** *Crucified Christ,* 1631, oil on canvas, 248 x 169 cm (Prado, Madrid) 15 E, D; **139.** *Las Meninas,* 1656, oil on canvas, 318 x 276 cm (Prado, Madrid) 25 E, D; **140.** *The Spinners,* 1657, oil on canvas, 220 x 289 cm (Prado, Madrid) 17 E; **141.** *The Toilet of Venus at the Mirror,* 1645–48, oil on canvas, 122.5 x 175 cm (National Gallery, London) 41 E, D; **142.** *View of Saragossa,* 1647, oil on canvas, 181 x 331 cm (Prado, Madrid) 7 E.